DISNEY

ENCANTO

NIGHTMARES AND SUEÑOS

DISNEY
ENCANTO
NIGHTMARES
AND SUEÑOS

By
Alex Segura

DISNEY PRESS
Los Angeles • New York

For information, address Disney Press, 1200 Grand Central Avenue, Glendale, California 91201.

Printed in the United States of America
First Hardcover Edition, December 2024
10 9 8 7 6 5 4 3 2 1
FAC-004510-24263

Library of Congress Control Number: 2024931813
ISBN 978-1-368-09790-1

Illustration by Grace Lee
Design by Winnie Ho
Composition and layout by Susan Gerber

Visit disneybooks.com

SUSTAINABLE FORESTRY INITIATIVE

Certified Sourcing

www.forests.org
SFI-01681

Logo Applies to Text Stock Only

For Guillermo and Lucia—
sueños realizados

PROLOGUE

I saw it all happen.

I saw my life flash before me. And I saw it changed forever—all in the span of a few moments. Before Encanto, there was a battle. A skirmish with that woman, Alma, her three children, and her husband—Pedro. I saw them huddled together, desperate to escape the evil that surrounded them. I saw the man—Pedro—fall. He didn't get up. I saw it all.

Why was I there? I've wondered this many times. How did I end up with my father's group, chasing these helpless people down? I long for the answer, but I don't expect to get it. Still, I remember it all. Every detail. The wind whipping against my face. The tears clouding my vision. The family's screams of pain and fear.

I saw the magic then. Bright, powerful. It swept Papi away. Swept his friends away. In an instant. One minute they were there—next to me. Then there was a flash. Then nothing. The sound of the wind ringing in my ears.

I was alone. My father was gone. His friends were, too. Where were they? How could I find them?

I wandered for what felt like a long time. I followed the broken family from a distance, aware even then that I should not be seen. Should not be connected to this dark, deadly event. If I was going to be alone—for quite a while—I needed to lurk in the shadows. To be invisible. From everyone.

But especially from the Madrigal family. I had to hide in the Encanto. Hide in plain sight. And plot my own journey to freedom—and family.

PART I
WE HAVE TO TALK ABOUT BRUNO

Excerpt from Julieta Madrigal's Diary

I feel a great weight on me, but I'm not sure why.

I should be happy. I should be content. But something seems to be eating at me.

Pepa has found her partner in Félix. I am happy for her—and happy we get to welcome him into the family. The love everyone feels for them is so strong, it almost overshadows what happened.

But my heart goes out to Bruno, as it always does. Our sweet brother is so well-intentioned that we often forget he has feelings, too. And those feelings can be hurt. I felt and saw it in real time on Pepa's wedding day.

He was only trying to help. But he inadvertently hurt those he loved.

He didn't mean to ruin the wedding. Didn't mean to suggest the weather would be bad. He was just being honest. He did what he's always done—told the truth. But it all went sideways. When things like this go wrong, especially with family, they linger. Poor Bruno.

Yes, these are the kinds of things that can fester. Things that in the moment seem resolved but end up getting infected. I know Bruno is tormented by what's going on, but what he did was merely use his gift in the way he's used to.

But time somehow smooths even the bumpiest events, and over the last few days, I've felt it. An ease that I'd thought long gone. I hope everything stays calm. I hope this lull isn't just a respite, but the beginning of a long stretch of peace and happiness for all of us. Ay Dios. I know we deserve it.

After everything Mami went through—to get us here, to build this town that protects us—she also deserves some peace.

And it seems like we're there.

But then why do I feel like we're not on a plateau, but about to fall over a steep cliff?

I need to go. Agustín scraped his leg badly and I promised him a warm soup. More soon.

CHAPTER ONE

Bruno Madrigal let out a long, meandering yawn. He squinted slightly as a glimmer of sunlight snuck into his bedroom through the shutters—the part that wasn't covered by the stacks of musty books and drawing paper, a winding pile reaching high up toward the ceiling like a spiral staircase. Bruno's room was packed—loaded with books, knickknacks, trinkets, and little things he picked up on any given day. It was his safe place, where he found peace, surrounded by the world as he wished to see it. But now the sun was creeping in.

Bruno wasn't sure what time it was, but he felt rested and relaxed—feelings that would soon fade once he got outside and started to wander Casita, the home he shared with his mami and hermanitas. The anxiety started to creep in—slowly at first, then spreading over his entire body.

Bruno caught a glimpse of himself in a tall mirror he'd propped up against the far wall of his room, most of it obscured by books and papers. He was tall, lanky even—with wide, somber eyes and a sharp nose. He tilted his head as his eyes scanned the reflection.

Who am I? Who is Bruno?

He was generally happy, Bruno thought. Or he was supposed to be. But the happiness he felt now— or thought he felt—was different from the pure, unfiltered kind he remembered from when he was a child. Not burdened by worries or anxiety. Not weighed down by his gift and the expectations that came with it. More innocent times.

But then his gift came. His visions solidified—at first as vague ideas. But as Bruno got older, wiser, his peeks into the future became more concrete and defined. He couldn't avoid them. And that childish happiness hardened into an adult need to survive. As the happiness had faded, he had to think about being happy—had to talk himself into it.

Bruno had never thought of these things as part of a greater whole when the visions first appeared when he was a child. Everyone's story—everyone's *life*—was different. A unique path in a zigzag series of paths. Bruno just happened to have a special gift that let him see a few steps down the line. And like clockwork, whenever Bruno talked to someone— whenever a resident of Encanto came to him in the hopes of learning what was next—it was always good. A positive bit of health news. A gift. A new addition to the family. Even little things—a nice dinner that evening, a rainbow on the walk home from work, a beautiful song playing. It was all nice. Bruno was seen, in Encanto, as a beacon of hope— like the candle itself. Like his beloved mother, Alma. Bruno was a sign that things were going to be more than all right. They were going to be great.

Then things changed. Bruno's gift changed. Everything felt rougher now, more intense.

But that was growing up, wasn't it? As far as anyone in the town was concerned, Bruno Madrigal was a happy guy. He was in a loving home. He wanted for very little. He had a family. His bare feet touched the floor of his room now, and he took in a long breath and remembered.

It came in a quick flood of visions and words: Pepa's wedding.

Bruno, along with his hermanas, Julieta and Pepa, was a triplet. They lived in the small closed-off town of Encanto, in a magical house they all lovingly referred to as Casita. On their shared fifth birthday, each of the Madrigal children was granted a magical gift. Pepa, excitable and crackling with energy, gained the power to generate and control the weather with her moods. Julieta, with her thoughtful eyes and warm smile, could heal others' ills with food. Bruno, by his estimation, got the short straw: he had visions. Dreamlike peeks into the future. At first, he didn't understand. For a short time, his mami, Alma, couldn't figure out what Bruno's gift even was. Bruno remembered the pained expression on his mami's somber face, her heavy eyes straining to figure out what was going on. Bruno recalled her stout, tiny frame moving from room to room, a kinetic energy propelling her during those uncertain times. Would it be that bad if he didn't have a gift? Bruno had asked. Alma didn't reply, which was enough of a response in and of itself.

But over the subsequent months, it became very

clear to Bruno that he'd gained something unique. It was an additive to an already joyous childhood, spent exploring every corner of Encanto and playing with his siblings and friends. Bruno's gift was a novelty to him as a child, hardening and defining in his mind only as he got older. Even then, it seemed to spring to the front of his mind only randomly. That changed around his eleventh birthday, like everything else. Bruno was feeling different. Older. More mature. And like his very being, his gift seemed to mature, too—to become more focused.

It had hit him as he walked through the small garden near Casita's main entrance, crouching down to look at a lovely sunflower that had cropped up over the previous few days. In Bruno's eyes, though, there was no flower—just a wilted stump. He remembered backing away in fear, unsure of what he was seeing. Then he had run. When he had wandered by the spot a few days later, his vision had come true. The flower was gone—wilted and dead.

Had he caused the flower to die? Bruno, not even a teenager, didn't fully understand. Could this gift—which had only been floating in the background of his mind for most of his life—actually do much more? Had his vision just come true coincidentally? But the moment opened the door, and soon, whenever Bruno had a flash—whether it was something minor, like a tear in Julieta's dress or an apple cart in the plaza tipping over, or something major, like Señor Bustamante falling ill—the vision would come true. Bruno, even at such a young age, couldn't deny what was happening. He could see the future. Good and bad. And he would never be that joyous, innocent boy again.

Pepa's wedding would fall under the *bad* category.

It was supposed to be a magical time. Pepa and Félix had spent months planning the event, with the help of Julieta and Alma. The entire town was abuzz about the festivities, and everyone who could turn out did. As far as anyone knew, it was set to be a beautiful sunny day—the perfect kind of weather for a wedding, especially one as magical as this. Alma's first child to be married.

Supposed to be.

Bruno understood his gift, knew what it could do. But he didn't always connect with others. The filters that many people had in place—the ones that gave them pause and helped them pick up on the social cues others were giving off—didn't always click into place for Bruno, and the wedding was one of those times.

He felt the warm breeze hit his face as he walked toward the church. Pepa's eyes were glowing with joy, but also anxious. Had Bruno been able to not just see that but truly *see* it, he would've probably kept his mouth shut. But Bruno had never been able to process these things. That, coupled with his gift, made for some awkward moments, to say the least.

"Looks like rain," he'd said. There wasn't a cloud in the sky. The sun was beating down on them. Everyone was joyous and laughing. It felt like it would be a beautiful day forever. There was no evidence of rain, the kind of clue or tip that would alert a regular person to bad weather. But Bruno saw things differently. And through his gift, it did look like rain. But it wasn't in the present. And it wasn't anything other people could see.

Bruno's gift propelled his mind's eye forward— creating visions of what was to come. Sometimes seconds in the future, often further down the line. But he knew one thing at that moment—in a short amount of time, it would rain.

Pepa wasn't keen on that. Bruno could still hear her shrill tone in response: "How could you *say that?*" the last two words dragging on like the final note in a long concierto.

It *had* rained, Bruno thought as he vividly remembered the event while slipping into a clean shirt and baggy khaki shorts. He'd been right. Why didn't Pepa understand then, or before, that this was Bruno's gift? Seeing the future.

"¡Bruuuuuuno? ¿Dónde estás, mijo? ¡Bruuuuno!"

His mami's words echoed through Casita, up from the house's spacious kitchen and through his closed door. Bruno Madrigal had to face the world. He had to be part of the community and society his family had created.

It was his duty.

Even if it was the last thing he wanted to do.

CHAPTER
TWO

Bruno felt heavy. Not heavy in the literal sense, mind you. Just weighed down.

Was it sadness? He wasn't sure. He couldn't really process the gray clouds that seemed to hover over him lately, the deep ache that he often ignored. Which he was currently doing.

He sped through Casita. Bruno knew the house better than anyone else—because he'd explored it in detail. Unlike his twins, Bruno loved spending most of his time at home. Loved wandering the winding corners and back doors. Marveled at the curious hutches and crawl spaces that seemed to filter through the house like a giant, complicated web. It was Bruno's safe space. A way to hide and think and escape the bustle and noise of the tiny town of

Encanto. Even Bruno had to come out occasionally, though.

But he didn't have to be seen.

And sometimes, he didn't *want* to be seen. Not by his hermanas, not by the neighbors, and certainly not by Mami. He could tell when their concern gauge was red, when the women in his life were conspiring to corner him and ask what was going on. This was one of those times, and Bruno couldn't deal with it.

He could still hear Mami's call as he tiptoed down the steps and sped out the front door of Casita—could almost feel Julieta's concerned look envelop him. He knew Mami meant well. She always did. But this wasn't the time. He didn't need anyone. Didn't want to relive the wedding—Pepa's angry look, the gasp of surprise from Félix, the rumble of storm clouds as if on cue. He just wished it hadn't happened—wished he'd been able to usher that vision of rain away and replace it with some-thing nicer, sunnier. And so what if it would have been proven wrong? At least people wouldn't have blamed *him*, right?

It was moments like these—moments that

seemed to occur with increasing regularity for Bruno—when he longed for his father, Pedro. Wondered what his life would've been like had his father lived.

Bruno let out a long sigh as he made a quick left down a side street. He felt an ache in his heart as he realized his only real knowledge of his father came from the images he saw on the walls of Casita, or the stories Mami shared when she was feeling nostalgic. Even then, with a pasted-together idea of who Pedro was, Bruno could see his vision of his father fading. Pedro's facial features were growing blurrier. Bruno was losing what little tether he had to his papi.

But there was something else now, too, Bruno realized. He spun around, taking a few quick steps backward as he looked—toward Casita—at the path he'd just walked. Had it been simply a feeling? A strange sense that something—no, *someone*—was behind him?

Someone was watching him?

Bruno shook it off and turned back around, waving at Señor Pinnelas, who was lugging what seemed to be a hefty toolbox. Bruno looked—his stare lingering on the man. Bruno felt a familiar tingle, and suddenly his vision blurred slightly. He still saw Señor Pinnelas, but now the older man was crouching down, screaming in anguish. The box he had so carefully carried was now on his hand, crushing his fingers. Behind him was a dark shape—about Bruno's height, but hard to make out. He could hear them laughing, though.

Bruno opened his mouth. He wanted to warn Señor Pinnelas, who had always been kind to him. But then his mind flashed back to Pepa's wedding. To the stricken look on her face when he'd merely said the weather might go sour.

But surely his neighbor would want to know to be vigilant? To be cautious? Or would Bruno be doing more harm than good?

He was talking before his mind had been made up. This happened a lot.

"Look out for that heavy toolbox, amigo," Bruno said, the dark shape still haunting his mind. Bruno let out a nervous laugh as a capper to his warning.

Pinnelas's eyes widened and the older man backed up slowly. Bruno watched as he set the toolbox down carefully and continued to back away.

"¿Qué dices, Bruno?" he said, slightly above a whisper, eyes still wide with fear. "Have I not been kind to you, mijo? Are you cursing me now?"

A curse?

Bruno had never thought of his gift that way—certainly not as a curse on others. But was his own gift a curse on himself?

"N-no, Señor Pinnelas, claro que no . . ." Bruno stammered. "Um, let me help you with that toolbox, okay? There's nothing to worry about. It's just that—"

But before Bruno could finish his thought, Pinnelas was halfway down the block, muttering to himself.

Bruno wanted to chase after him, to convince the man that his powers were just a gift, not a curse. But to what end? For a long time, when he was younger, Bruno had prided himself on his ability. Felt like he was being helpful. Alerting friends, family, neighbors to the good news that awaited them. And the visions were received with joy and anticipation. Bruno could do no wrong. People would seek him out in the hopes of capturing a bit of his gift, of being touched by a slight jolt of good fortune. But what had changed? Bruno wondered. It seemed like lately, the news was rarely—if ever—good. Visions of people tripping and falling. Bad weather. Accidents. Arguments. Destruction. Doom. They were everywhere, replacing the joy and bright future Bruno had taken for granted.

Was it his fault?

Had his own darkening mood started to seep into his gift? Could he even trust himself to see what was happening?

"But that's the thing," he muttered to himself, turning toward the town square, hoping to get lost in the crowds and sounds of Encanto. "If my visions were wrong, I'd doubt myself."

But he was never wrong.

As Bruno approached the center of town—surrounded by stores; booths selling flavorful foods, toys, and anything else you could imagine; musicians playing ballads of lands long forgotten; and the sounds of children playing—he caught sight of Julieta, his twin, looking calm and serene as she made her way through the hustle and bustle of Encanto. Everyone seemed to either step aside and watch her with reverence or try to catch her eye, eager to feel the touch or gain the attention of Julieta Madrigal, one of the three siblings. They loved her. They talked to her about food—what she was cooking—and then, naturally, about what ailed them. Julieta was always patient and kind. She told Mari Aspuru to come by later for some arroz y frijoles. She nodded patiently as Eduardo Escala recounted his latest woes before inviting him to Casita for some caldo de pollo. It was like clockwork. Bruno hung back and just watched in wonder at his sister's powerful command of the crowd, like royalty, and how the people seemed to surge after her—in the way Bruno remembered them surging after him.

But those days were over, Bruno realized.

As much as they loved Julieta and her healing treats, as much as they respected Pepa—a respect that, in turn, made Pepa's own gift better for Encanto—they feared Bruno.

And there was nothing he could do about it.

No matter how much Bruno tried, how desperately he curated his visions, how thoughtful he was about what he shared—he could not make people like him. The rumor mill had revved up. The gossip was piping hot. If someone got a vision from Bruno, it was bad news—and few things were hated more than bad news. One of those things? The person bearing it.

Bruno let out a long sigh, spun on his heel, and walked away from the town square. He needed to be alone—for a while.

CHAPTER
THREE

Bruno thought back to the wedding. It should've been a day of celebration. Of joy and happiness. And it was, eventually. But not as far as Bruno was concerned.

Everyone loved Félix. He was kind, doted on Pepa, and was so eager and excited to join the family. Bruno had never seen Pepa like this—her happiness unbridled and pure, whatever sharp edges she used to have smoothed over by the pink cloud of love. He thought about this as he knotted his tie, staring at his reflection in the mirror in his room. It would be a special day, Bruno had told himself. It had to be.

Bruno, finally dressed but running late, stepped outside of the house. The sun seemed to dominate the sky—bright and orange, creating a warmth and light that felt appropriate. Beautiful weather on what was sure to be a beautiful day, Bruno thought.

He was happy for Pepa, Bruno thought as he made his way toward the ceremony. She'd spent weeks, months, planning it all—making sure every detail was perfect. She'd struggled with the idea of having it outside, unsure if the weather would hold. But everyone—even that strange man Francisco Padilla—had assured her that the skies would stay clear. Bruno hoped they were right.

As Bruno wove through the crowd, he saw Félix first. The entire village was there, standing outside in the blazing sun, soaking up the energy and love that was building for both Pepa and Félix.

He looked nervous, was Bruno's first thought. The usually easygoing Félix seemed jittery and worried, pacing on the cobblestone steps that made up Encanto's central square.

"Bruno, hey, it's good to see you," Félix said, approaching Bruno and pulling him in for a tight hug. "I was getting a little worried."

"You know I wouldn't miss this for the world, Félix," Bruno said, forcing a smile. A smile would help calm him down, Bruno thought. "Beautiful day, too."

"Not a cloud in the sky," Félix said, his eyes distant.

Bruno waved a hand in front of Félix's face, snapping his future brother-in-law out of his self-imposed daze.

"Where is mi hermanita, anyway?"

Félix blinked a few times and then motioned toward the center of the square. It didn't take long for Bruno to pinpoint where Pepa was. The tiny gray cloud hovering over her head did the work there. Bruno thought he saw a quick burst of rain trickle down.

She looked beautiful, in a lovely white dress, her hair made up in a way Bruno had never seen before. She was radiant, he thought. But also anxious. Stressed. And Bruno knew what happened when Pepa was unhappy. Her gift was tied to the weather, but that gift, in turn, was tied to her mood. If she was mad, thunder and lightning were likely. If she was calm and serene, the skies would be clear and placid.

"Is she okay?" Bruno asked Félix.

"I hope so, Bruno," Félix said with a shrug before returning to his pacing. "We're just getting ready—it's almost time."

The crowd seemed to be at a maximum. Bruno felt like he was surrounded by everyone he'd ever met—a who's who of Encanto, Casita, and his entire life. Mami. Julieta. His friend Roberto. His classmates Heidi and Annalise. Even in the distance, Francisco Padilla was looking on. This was the event of the season. Everyone was watching.

And, it seemed, Pepa knew this—could feel it.

Bruno's throat tightened as he approached his sister, who was pacing in a tight circle—probably etching a ring with her feet—her eyes down, the gray cloud chasing her like a soggy shadow. Bruno wanted to help her, wanted to soothe his sister's anxiety so she could enjoy the day—the same way everyone else here would. What could he do?

The vision arrived then—brief, but powerful. Of a storm, rain pelting down on Encanto. Bruno shook his head and tried to fight the vision off, but it lingered as he walked toward his sister. Why now, he wondered? The storm finally disappeared in Bruno's vision, and he saw Pepa again, though the force of the vision now loomed over him like a long shadow.

But he had to help Pepa. He steeled himself as he placed a hand on Pepa's thin shoulder, and she turned to face him, relief washing over her as she recognized who was greeting her. He forced another smile, trying to push the vision of the rainstorm out of his mind.

"Oh, Bruno, gracias a Dios you're here," Pepa said, a wide grin replacing the scowl that had been on her face moments before. "I was just about to send Mami to—"

"Looks like rain," Bruno blurted, unable to dance around the thoughts pounding in his skull like a giant hammer trying to find a wall's weak spot. He couldn't help himself. He didn't have the kind of filters others had, he knew this. But he'd hoped, for once, he could just keep his mouth shut.

Pepa's face looked stricken, like she'd stepped into something unexpected. The shock turned to surprise. Soon it was anger.

"How . . . how could you *say that?*" Pepa asked, taking a few hurried steps back from her brother. Bruno watched as the tiny cloud above Pepa grew—the gray shape turning darker and floating up. Bruno watched as the gray-and-black clouds merged with the bright sky, spreading and covering what was once a beautiful day. "You . . . saw the rain? You saw it would rain today? It's a prophecy?"

Bruno raised his hands in defense, trying desperately to talk to his sister—but it was too late.

Pepa was storming away, the cloud no longer a singular, personal thing. It was the sky now. Thunder crackled. Rain followed immediately. Bruno heard Julieta call for Mami to get the umbrellas, then the scurrying of desperate feet as people sought cover from the downpour.

First a light rain, then the kind of rain that felt like it was alive—a ponderous, heavy rain—with winds screaming in the distance. Un huracán, Bruno thought.

"How could you do this to me?" Pepa screamed, not at her brother—she wasn't even looking at him now—but at the sky. Her voice loud, angry, as if her throat was being ripped out with the words.

And all of Encanto was watching Bruno, waiting for him to respond.

"How could you do this to me?"
Not a cloud in the sky.

⊚⊚⊚⊚⊚

The storm raged for a while. Bruno managed to get cover near Casita, hidden behind a fruit stand and a carriage. He was still soaked—the hurricane winds and rain pelting Encanto like nothing he'd ever seen. He tried to think over what had happened. To replay every step to himself to figure out what he'd done wrong. What he could have done differently.

He hadn't called forth the vision on purpose—he couldn't control them. Though once it started, he'd assumed it would be nice. The weather seemed impenetrable. But Pepa had already been stressed—las nubes were already forming above her. Had he nudged them along?

Pepa hadn't wanted to hear about any clouds. She didn't want his visions—good or bad. She'd wanted to be reassured. Supported. Loved. Not jabbed at.

He slapped a palm to his forehead. Why couldn't he understand? Bruno thought. Why couldn't he know, inside, what to do or say, and when? Why was it so hard for him—when it seemed so easy for everyone else?

He tried to look out—through the rain, through the people rushing to move the food, the tables, the chairs, everything, out of the way—to see what was happening. But he couldn't see Pepa. Couldn't find Félix, either. He wanted to run. They surely hated him now, Bruno thought, the wetness on his face more than rain. He was about to stand up when he heard voices.

"He told me my fish would die," someone said. It was Señora Pezmuerto, her voice sharp—a gossiping tone. "And the next day? Dead."

Bruno wanted to speak—to clarify—about how she'd pressured him, asked repeatedly to find out the fate of her already sick fish. But he didn't. To what end? Bruno thought.

Then another voice—a man's, deeper, crankier. Osvaldo.

"He said I'd grow a gut, and next thing you know . . ." Osvaldo said. There was a pause. Bruno assumed the older man was showcasing the shape of his belly.

Bruno couldn't handle any more. He moved out of his hiding spot—relished the surprised reaction from Pezmuerto and Osvaldo for a brief moment, then remembered why he was even hiding. He'd disrupted Pepa's wedding—perhaps irrevocably. Bruno felt the rain pelting his face. Heard the rumble of thunder so loud it seemed like Encanto was shaking.

He wanted to run to Pepa, to apologize and explain everything to her.

But would she listen?

Another crack of thunder.

He shook his head and walked back to Casita, his entire body soaked by the storm of his own creation.

CHAPTER

FOUR

"¿Bruno, pero qué te pasa?"

The words seemed to jump on Bruno as he sat under a tree about half a mile away from the center of town, reminiscing about the disastrous wedding from a few days earlier. He didn't have to turn around to figure out who was talking to him.

Roberto.

His friend's powerful hands gripped his shoulders, and a great relief washed over him. Bruno had few friends in this world. He loved his family, but that always felt fraught in the ways families sometimes were. It was different with friends. And Roberto was a true friend.

Bruno stood up and embraced his tall companion. Roberto pulled Bruno in tighter. It was good to see him, Bruno thought. It'd been a while since they'd hung out. The entire Madrigal family had been so distracted by Pepa's wedding that Bruno had been unable to escape to just relax and spend time with his friend. But now that the wedding was over—for better or worse—Bruno longed for some kind of normalcy.

"What do you mean?" Bruno asked as he stepped back from the hug.

"I saw you talking to Señor Pinnelas, Bruno," Roberto said, a look of concern on his sharp features. "It was like you scared him. What did you say? I always took that man to be fearless."

Bruno shrugged. A familiar shame hit him. Even here, with his best friend, it was strong.

"Did it happen again?" Roberto asked, placing a hand on his shoulder again.

Bruno pulled back and shook his head.

"No, I mean, yes, but it's fine—I'm used to it."

"You don't have to be," Roberto said, matching Bruno's step back. "I can help you. I can help you figure out what to do. Give you advice."

Bruno shook his head again, harder this time. He didn't want help. He just wanted to be alone. Seeing

Roberto had been a relief, but now it seemed like more work. More to avoid. What if he had another vision, now? Of Roberto hurt? Of people he knew in danger? Of anything?

"Bruno, I'm your friend. You're having a bad time. That's what friends are for, no?" Roberto said as he sat down. He motioned for Bruno to sit next to him, which he did. Then Roberto wrapped an arm around him and gave Bruno another hug. "There you go. Don't you feel better? Tell me what's going on, hermano."

Bruno did, recounting the wedding and its aftermath—capped with his encounter with Pinnelas. Bruno was surprised how relieved he felt just talking about everything. Although he couldn't bring himself to mention the dark figure, unloading the rest helped, a little bit. Bruno felt less alone. But it wasn't enough.

"It's your gift, isn't it?" Roberto asked.

Bruno nodded.

"People want to see the future," Bruno said, hesitating slightly with each word. "They don't understand, though, that their future isn't always good. Sometimes it might rain. Sometimes you might trip or fall. Sometimes you might lose something you cherish. . . ."

"People want the good news," Roberto said with a nod. "But you can't control that."

"Right," Bruno said, his voice excited. Finally, someone was understanding him. "And I can't explain that each time, you know? I don't have a disclaimer on my forehead: visions may not be great."

Bruno saw Roberto rubbing his chin. Could almost see the gears turning in his head. Before he could ask his friend what he was thinking, Roberto's eyes widened and he looked at Bruno with a smile.

"I've got an idea, Bruno—but you need to trust me. You need to be open to changing, well, everything," Roberto said. "Let's go to Casita."

CHAPTER

FIVE

Alma was waiting for the boys when they returned to the house, full of excited energy and fun. The mood shifted the moment Bruno saw his mami.

"¡Bruno, adónde fuiste? I was calling you all morning," Alma scolded as Bruno and Roberto walked up the front steps. "You can't just—"

"I'm sorry, Mami," Bruno said, hanging his head slightly.

This was common for them. His mother, as caring and thoughtful as she was, often laid into him directly for some perceived mistake or slight. Bruno had just become accustomed to apologizing immediately to get past the discomfort, whether he believed he was in the wrong or not.

Alma stepped forward and placed a hand on Bruno's cheek.

"¿Qué te pasa, mijo?" she asked, tilting her head to catch Bruno's distant gaze. "Don't worry about your sister, okay? She loves you. No matter what. It was her wedding day, okay? She was—"

"I know, Mami," Bruno said, still not meeting her eyes. "Pero . . ."

"¿Pero qué, Bruno?" Alma asked, leaning forward a bit, as if straining to hear some hidden truth. "You know you can talk to me. . . ."

Before Bruno could respond, Roberto spoke.

"Hola, Señora Madrigal," he said, his voice joyous and relaxed. "We were just going up to Bruno's room to hang out."

Alma opened her mouth to reply, but no words came out. It was as if the presence of Roberto made her less inclined to talk to her son, who was clearly in distress.

"Bueno, that sounds good," she said slowly. "Roberto, you're welcome to stay for dinner, too, if it's all right with your family."

Bruno watched as Roberto nodded in agreement. He knew his friend appreciated the offer, and that he longed to be a part of not only the community—but the Madrigal home.

Bruno knew Roberto had a loving adoptive home—he lived with Señora Enríquez; her husband, Daniel; and their children. She was an old friend of Alma Madrigal's and one of the kindest people in Encanto. Roberto was loved and well cared for, he knew—but Bruno could also sense a longing for something in his friend, an idea of where he came from, perhaps? Bruno wasn't sure.

This was all his own speculation. He hadn't asked Roberto about it. Wouldn't dare, really. It was none of his business. In fact, he found it kind of interesting that Roberto—charming, garrulous, and friendly Roberto—might have any secret hopes or dreams. Nothing seemed to faze him. He was constantly cheerful and easygoing. So different from Bruno and his varying moods. But he also never seemed to go anywhere. Bruno had met his family, but it was a rare occurrence. Roberto was much more likely to come to Casita or intercept Bruno in the village. Encanto was a tiny town—everyone knew almost everything there was to know about all the others. Sure, it led to a lot of gossip and chitchat, but it also meant that people were around to help as needed. Yet Bruno had never heard a thing about Roberto's family of origin, despite having been close friends with him for the past year. He'd been drawn to Roberto, a boy with no real roots in Encanto, because he felt a kinship with him—that they were both outsiders cautiously walking among the people. The revelation that Roberto had lost his birth family somehow only made Bruno long to be closer to him.

Encanto was different in many ways from your typical town—magic notwithstanding. But its makeup wasn't that far afield from what Bruno understood to be "normal." Families could be any combination—two parents, one parent, communal families. The spectrum existed, Bruno knew. Who was Bruno to speculate about what his friend needed or longed for? he thought.

"¿En qué piensas, Bruno?" Roberto asked as he sped by him up the stairs to Bruno's room.

What *was* he thinking about?

He watched Roberto reach the top of the stairs and pivot left toward Bruno's cavernous room. Then his mind went somewhere else.

It was a vision. But not a vision of Roberto. Or of anyone else he knew. And it wasn't new.

He felt his body fall forward. He hugged himself, gripping his own arms tightly as he sat down on the steps.

Over the past week Bruno Madrigal had experienced the vision a half dozen times. Each time, it was identical—lasting the exact same amount of time and sending the same images through his mind, like an electric shock. And each time, he felt shattered by the time the vision was over.

He thought he could hear Roberto's voice in the background, a concerned tone in it. But he couldn't be sure.

Bruno could almost feel the warmth on his face. Could almost feel the smoke slapping his skin. Could hear the crackle of fire. Bruno could make out the silhouette—of a tall figure standing before him, their back to Bruno. The person was looking toward something—toward the burning structure that had once, long ago, been Bruno's home. Bruno could also hear laughter. A low, thrumming laugh that sounded otherworldly and menacing, like a hyena's bark—devious and jovial, with a hint of darkness. The sound cut through the crackling of the flame, the crashing of pieces of wood, the panicked screams of Bruno's own family and neighbors as they, too, looked on—as they witnessed Bruno's worst nightmare, now a vision preordaining a future he couldn't even try to change. A future he dreaded with every fiber of his being.

Casita was on fire, and Bruno could do nothing to stop it.

CHAPTER
SIX

Roberto's voice brought him back. A desperate cry. It pulled Bruno from the vision, a surprise but also a reprieve.

"What happened, Bruno?" Roberto asked, eyes wide. His friend was worried, Bruno could see. He appreciated it. But he wasn't ready to talk about it—not now.

Bruno waved his hand, trying to seem casual.

"No, nothing, don't worry," Bruno said. He could tell, though, that his words were having the opposite effect. Roberto was more worried now.

The visions were haunting Bruno.

It happened all the time, Bruno thought. But it also seemed to be happening more frequently.

There was a stretch, a few years, when Bruno had looked forward to these kinds of exchanges. These moments with friends, family, strangers—where he could give them a slight peek at what was to come. A present. A treat. Bruno lived for the wide-eyed expectation and rush of joy these people received when he shared a vision with them. When he confirmed to them that, yes, things would get better. That they would have good news on the horizon. That things would not only be okay—but they would be great.

Until they weren't.

Although the downward turn had started long before Pepa's wedding, that was the capper, to Bruno. That was the moment when he realized it was more than one singular event, or a series of unrelated tidbits of bad news. No, this was now a trend, and Bruno had to come to terms with what his gift had become. It was no longer always a pleasant surprise that could be doled out with glee. It was now the kind of gift Bruno had to be judicious about using. Every interaction, every vision, was a roll of the dice. It could just as likely go sour as sweet. But Bruno wasn't built for that. Bruno didn't have the filter in place that would stop him from sharing what he saw, and most people didn't understand that.

Take Claudia Mijares, the town doctor. She was healthy. Middle-aged. The mother of three children and married to Encanto's best carpenter, Alfredo. Claudia had known Bruno and his sisters since they were small children, at the earliest point of the town's life. She knew them, knew their gifts, and loved them like family. At checkups, she'd playfully ask Bruno what the future held for her, and each time, Bruno would dutifully pretend to look into the future—and report back to his doctor. It was always good. A life saved. A warm hug from her daughter. A tasty treat from a patient. Some were big, some were small, but all were great. Dr. Claudia loved Bruno and cherished their time together. Until she didn't.

It was a few months back. Bruno had come in for his yearly checkup. Dr. Claudia said everything was fine, that Bruno wasn't a kid anymore, but a man. She was proud of what he'd become. He was healthy, growing, and thriving. Bruno appreciated the news, but he couldn't shake a simmering anxiety. He knew what Dr. Claudia was going to ask. He knew he'd always foretold good news. But would that hold? he wondered.

"Dime, Bruno, mi niño—what news do you have for me today?" she'd asked, her back to him in her small examining room. "What does the future hold?"

Bruno swallowed hard. He closed his eyes, wincing slightly. He hoped it would be good, but even the frequency of the visions themselves was a sign of something greater—and Bruno had felt a strange change within himself, a textural change in how he interacted with his gift. He couldn't explain it. But it was coursing through every part of him. Something was different lately. But he hoped that it wouldn't affect this moment. He loved Dr. Claudia. He loved her family. He didn't want to let her down.

But he didn't want to lie to her, either.

"I see . . . I see you coming home," Bruno started. "The house . . . the house is empty. No, wait. The children are there. But your husband . . . he's gone. There's a note—"

Before Bruno could continue, Dr. Claudia spun around, her face pale, eyes and mouth open wide.

"When? When does this happen?"

The vision was broken. Bruno didn't know. He just knew what he'd seen.

"I'm not sure, Doctora, pero—"

"Where is he? Where is Alfredo?" Dr. Claudia asked, leaning forward, placing a hand on each of Bruno's shoulders. She was gripping them now, her expression curious and . . . angry?

"Doctora, I can only tell you what I saw. . . ."

Dr. Claudia didn't respond. Before Bruno could say anything else, she was gone, her footsteps clattering down the office hallway.

Bruno was never a patient of Dr. Claudia's again. He'd heard, through the Encanto gossip mill, that Alfredo had left, moved to the other side of town. That they had decided to part ways.

When Bruno had tried to return for a follow-up, Dr. Claudia's secretary told him to book an appointment with another doctor. That Claudia was no longer available. Bruno did so, trying his best not to think it was all connected. Though of course, it was. Bruno Madrigal wasn't foolish. He saw after the fact how his premonitions affected people. But he wasn't a liar, either. He couldn't see a vision, then tweak and twist it to fit what he thought the person wanted. Wouldn't that pervert the gift he'd received? Wouldn't that distort the magic coursing through the town?

The last time he saw Dr. Claudia was at the town farmers market a few weeks later. He'd looked across the fruit cart and seen her examining an apple for bruises. She glanced up and Bruno almost backed away in fear. It was the same Dr. Claudia, of course—but she seemed broken. Sad. Shattered. Her expression no longer vibrant and idealistic, but muted and defeated. Who had done this to her? he wondered. But the answer popped into his mind before he could ask her.

He had done this.

She turned away from him, seemingly hoping to avoid conversation. He didn't press the issue. He watched as his childhood doctor shambled away, muttering to herself.

If that had been an isolated incident, he could've chalked it up to the law of averages. If you delivered news and ideas to people regularly, it wasn't always going to be great. For every rainbow there'd be a thunderstorm. For every reunion there'd be a loss. But this hadn't been isolated. It had just been first.

Hernán Otero was Bruno's age, though not in his grade at school. He had been one of his sister Julieta's many suitors. Bruno understood the hierarchy of Encanto. Though nothing like a traditional monarchy, the Madrigals were seen as the most powerful and beloved family in the town. And with Pepa, at that time, engaged to be married to Félix, and the wedding just a few days away, only Julieta remained in terms of eligible Madrigal brides. The line of potential suitors was long, even if it didn't literally wind around Casita. Hernán was strapping—tall, raven-haired, with glittering green eyes and a toothy smile that was debonair and bashful at once. Bruno barely knew Hernán, but he'd never heard a cross word about him. He was athletic, smart, and kind. Their mother, Alma, loved him, pointing to him as a perfect addition to the family. Not coincidentally, he started coming around Casita more and more. First to sit with Alma and share stories. Then to spend time with Julieta in the yard. Eventually, Bruno knew, he'd be coming to take his sister out— to build a bond between them.

But Julieta wasn't having it. Sure, Hernán checked all the boxes—but so what? She needed a spark. A connection. She wanted to actually *like* the person she was going to marry. She'd told their mother as much, and Bruno had spent many hours with his sister trying to manage her conflicting emotions over Hernán, the town's expectations, and her own feelings. Feelings that seemed to hover around someone else, someone Bruno knew well—Roberto.

Julieta wasn't sure what love was, or if she was feeling it. But the mysterious, handsome Roberto held more allure for her than did Hernán, who was nice and easy on the eyes but also a bit boring. She didn't dare tell their mother this, of course. Alma Madrigal was a practical, driven woman. Marriage was, of course, a partnership based on love. But it was a partnership. A pooling of resources meant to not only benefit each other but the family as a whole. Whoever Julieta married was also marrying the entire Madrigal clan. And Alma had made it clear—she liked Hernán for Julieta.

Bruno could see Julieta's conundrum. He liked Roberto, too. He was a character. Funny, energetic, and sporting the right amount of mystery. He was

also a good friend—an avid listener and thoughtful with his advice and insight. Bruno told Julieta
to follow her heart. She clutched his hand in
appreciation.

The next morning, Hernán had arrived for his
daily visit to Julieta. Bruno could tell that he was
confident and eager to make progress. That alone
didn't mean Hernán didn't care for his sister.
Julieta was wonderful. As beautiful inside as out,
and a kind, generous soul who could literally heal
with her food. If anyone would take over for Alma
when the time came, Bruno was certain it would be
Julieta—diplomatic, pensive, and quick-witted. So,
yes, Bruno understood that two things could be true
at one time—Hernán would see the inherent benefit
of marrying into the Madrigal family, and might
also love his sister. None of it mattered, though, if
Julieta didn't feel the same way.

Bruno opened the door and greeted Hernán.
They shook hands. Bruno didn't realize that their
dynamic would never be the same after that.

As soon as he felt Hernán's warm palm touch
his, Bruno saw a flash of light in his mind's eye.
Moments later, the bright light was replaced by

something else—a clearer image, of Hernán, angry and ashamed, storming away from Casita, cursing those standing in the doorway watching him leave. What had happened? Was this how Hernán would react to Julieta's rejection? Bruno couldn't let his sister experience this, he thought. He would bear the brunt if he had to.

"Hernán," Bruno said, the word coming out slowly. He could tell the other man had noticed what happened. But his expression seemed expectant and excited.

"What is it, Bruno? Do you see something? About me? About me and your sister?"

Bruno opened his mouth to respond, but his expression said more than his words ever could. He wasn't smiling—he must have looked downright scared, he knew. And Hernán reacted accordingly.

"It's bad, isn't it?" Hernán asked, his question laced with anger. "She doesn't like me, huh?"

"It's not that, Hernán, it's just that—"

Hernán wasn't having any of it. He backed away, shoving Bruno in the other direction.

Out of the corner of Bruno's vision, he saw his sister Julieta approach.

"Bruno?" she asked. "What's happening? Hernán?"

"This is your fault," Hernán said, each word a hiss, not even reacting to Julieta's appearance. "You did this. You never liked me, Bruno. You don't think I'm good enough for your sister. Well, you know what? You can have her, okay? You and your crazy powers can protect her from everyone. I want nothing to do with you!"

And Hernán stormed off, waving his arm back at Bruno in anger.

Bruno felt Julieta's hand on his arm—a gesture of concern and empathy. His sister, even not knowing what was happening, always defaulted to kindness. Especially toward Bruno. But in this case, he knew she was also feeling something else: great worry.

"What did you see, Bruno?"

Bruno couldn't respond. Couldn't vocalize the thoughts that had been broadcast in his mind so clearly.

The vision had immediately become reality. And another person now saw Bruno as a danger— a threat—to not only themselves but the entire town.

"What did you see?"

CHAPTER
SEVEN

Bruno sat in his usual spot—in the far-left corner of the tiny classroom where he went to school each day. He liked sitting there. Liked seeing what everyone else was doing. Also liked how, if he was quiet enough, he could blend into the class itself. Even disappear if he needed to. It happened more often than not, he realized.

It was impossible for anyone not to know who Bruno was. The Madrigals were at the center of Encanto, and Alma Madrigal was not only the family's matriarch but the core of the village as well. People came to her for help. They followed what was happening with the family. Whether Bruno liked it or not, he was in the public eye. But thankfully, at school, it seemed like fewer and fewer people were

interested in what he was doing if he didn't do anything to catch their attention.

Ever since Pepa's wedding, Bruno had tried really
hard to fly out of sight and under the radar. Though
Pepa was still finishing up her last year in school,
her bond with Félix was powerful—strong enough
for their mami to okay the wedding. Pepa had made
it exceedingly clear she couldn't see herself with
anyone else, and Alma knew enough to listen to
her daughter. That was before. After the wedding,
Bruno tried his best not to even think about it—or
talk about it. There was no upside, he thought, to
drawing attention to himself. He hoped today would
be more of the same. He wondered how Roberto was
doing. He wanted to talk to him again—about what
happened with Hernán, about the wedding. About
his gift. But it would have to wait. Roberto was older
than Bruno and had already graduated. Bruno longed
for some time with his friend—with someone who
seemed to understand him. It took Bruno a long
time to make connections with people, to feel comfortable and happy with those he'd allow to become
friends. School, he thought, moved too fast for that.
You listened to the teacher, you did your work, you

laughed when someone made a joke—but there was no opportunity for meaningful connection. As much as he loved to read and learn, whenever he got to school, it was like a ticking clock. He wanted to get out, run back home, and lose himself in his room and world. He didn't want to be the center of attention, even if he couldn't help it.

He tried not to groan when Maximo sat next to him, giving Bruno a long glare, a humorless smile painted on his wide face. Maximo was a good kid, Bruno knew, but he also had a cruel and cutting sense of humor. The kind of thing that maturity and time usually dulled. But for now, he was a smart kid who liked to cut people down. Often, his main target was Bruno.

"Buenos días, Bruno," Maximo said, his voice rising slightly, imitating the teacher. "¿Cómo estás?"

"I'm fine, Maximo," Bruno said, his voice low and fast.

Heidi took the seat in front of Bruno and turned around to face him.

"Bruno, why do you always hide back here?" she said innocently, her glasses sliding down the bridge of her nose. Heidi was kind and smart. She reminded

Bruno of Pepa a bit in how she carried herself. She was confident and didn't seem to care what other people thought of her. It was a trait Bruno wished he could have for himself.

"I like this spot," Bruno said.

"He's a weirdo, Heidi," Maximo said. "No le hagas caso. He doesn't want to talk to us normal people. He's too busy running the town with his family."

Bruno opened his mouth to respond but was cut off by Heidi's quick words.

"Oh, please, Maximo. Encanto is basically, like, paradise," she said, scolding. "If Bruno has any part in that, we should be throwing a party for him."

Maximo shrugged and cracked open his text-book. History was their first subject. Bruno felt like the day was already getting away from him. Heidi patted Bruno on the arm.

"Don't listen to him. You know he just likes to jab at people," she said, turning back to face the teacher. "Weird is cool, trust me. No te preocupes, Bruno."

Bruno smiled as the teacher began to speak.

Class droned on, and Bruno was only half listen-ing. He had a lot on his mind, and school was not something he wanted to spend much time on. Normally he enjoyed the class itself—even if the other students made him uncomfortable. But today was different. He felt like he was on the edge of a steep cliff looking down, and he wasn't sure he knew how to back away. His mind kept shifting to Hernán's look of surprise and betrayal at Bruno's words. Then that look was replaced by another sharp expression: Pepa's, on her wedding day, when she was feeling blindsided and betrayed by Bruno's gift of prophecy.

But his gift was a good thing, Bruno told himself. Surely there was a way to convince everyone of this. To show them that what he had to offer the Encanto was positive, not something weird and creepy to be shunned and avoided.

A hand slammed on his desk and Bruno snapped to attention. He looked up to see Ramón, one of the other kids in his class, stifling a laugh as he slithered back to his seat across the classroom. The noise had startled the teacher, Señora Morales, who spun around and looked at Bruno.

"¿Qué pasó? What was that noise?" she asked, peering over her thick glasses. "Bruno? What's going on?"

Bruno could feel Ramón's eyes on him, the stare sharp and long from across the room. Screaming, threatening. *Go ahead, try it, Bruno. See what happens when you say my name to the teacher. See how that helps you.* Ramón hadn't said that, of course. But Bruno didn't need to hear the words to understand the message.

He cleared his throat.

"Nada, Señora Morales. I dropped my book," he said.

Bruno could tell the teacher didn't buy it but was also eager to move things along. She shrugged and turned around, jotting something on the chalkboard.

Bruno sighed. He turned to look at Ramón, who gave him a knowing nod before moving his attention to the teacher.

"You should've told on him," Heidi whispered, not looking back, just canting her head slightly so Bruno would notice she was talking to him. "Ramón sucks."

Bruno smiled as he looked down at his blank notebook page.

Heidi approached him as they exited the school. Bruno was already picking up speed, wondering if he could beat his record—home in less than fifteen minutes. That was out the window now that he was being ensnared by small talk, he thought.

"Hey, Bruno," Heidi said, bumping into him playfully. "You okay?"

"What? Oh, yes, I'm fine," Bruno said, nodding nervously. He hadn't expected the question. Hadn't really expected any conversation. This was usually his alone time. Or the beginning of it. "Just the usual classroom stuff, I guess."

"You don't realize how powerful you are," Heidi said as they walked through the town, not meeting his eyes, just looking ahead. "If you did, none of these bullies and jerks would intimidate you. Do you think someone like that Padilla guy gets scared by bullies? You don't have to be like everyone else. You don't have to let them scare you."

Bruno's throat went dry. The mention of Padilla—an outsider few in the town trusted but Bruno felt an affinity to—hit him hard. Was he like Padilla? An outcast who lurked on the edges of town, not to be trusted . . . or loved?

"Well, I'm not intimidated," Bruno said, not even believing his own words as he spoke them. But if he didn't, what was he admitting to? "I just don't, I dunno, don't want to get into a big thing with people."

Heidi turned to him.

"Bruno, you're a Madrigal. Your family founded this town. People know you have a gift and that you can see what's coming. You could look at Ramón and tell him he's going to wake up with a fish tail tomorrow and he'd never come back to school," she said with a short laugh. "You must understand that, right?"

Bruno nodded. He did understand that. But he'd never considered it the way Heidi explained.

"But that would be wrong," Bruno said.

"Would it?" Heidi asked. "Sometimes people need to be put in their place. Maybe a little scare would teach Ramón a lesson."

Heidi patted Bruno on the shoulder and smiled.

"I gotta go. My mami needs my help with some house stuff," she said. "I'll see you later, though. Think about what I said."

Bruno waved and watched as Heidi skipped toward her house.

He stopped and pondered her words. His gift was powerful, Bruno knew. He didn't take it for granted. It was definitely something that could be used for evil—to scare, intimidate, or hurt. But could the opposite be true, too?

He wasn't sure. His gift was such a wild card. Sometimes he just felt like the messenger of information that he couldn't manage himself and often didn't want.

Bruno didn't have much time to mull it over. He heard his name being called. He turned around to see a much-needed friendly face.

CHAPTER
EIGHT

"**A**re you sure that's what you saw?"

Roberto's question hung between them as they walked on the edge of town, the sounds and bustle of the village a distant echo. It was late afternoon. School was over, and Bruno needed a break. From the people, his world, his family—and, most important, his visions. But even here, hanging out with his best friend, he could not avoid his visions—or the anxiety that seemed to surround them.

"Of course I'm sure," Bruno said, his words tinged with annoyance. He knew Roberto didn't deserve this backlash, that it was self-directed more than anything. But Bruno couldn't help being annoyed. Why did the gifts his twins received seem so much more . . . palatable? Food, weather.

These were things that could be used for good. But Bruno's gift felt out of control. Like something he couldn't direct or manage. He witnessed his visions. He didn't determine them. He couldn't change the future he saw. Or . . . could he?

"I see it all the time, but each time it's a little different," Bruno said. "Like, today, I had this great sense of—I dunno, betrayal. Like someone was going to hurt us from within. I could see Encanto. It was like I'd zoomed out and could look down on the town. I could see everyone walking around, completely unaware of what was coming. Then a thick cloud—like a darkness, like a velvet cloth—fell over Encanto. And no matter what I said, or what everyone did, it couldn't be lifted. . . ."

Roberto placed a hand on Bruno's shoulder and turned to face him.

"What was it, Bruno?"

"Something—someone—had hurt the village, everyone in it," Bruno said, his voice cracking. "We were blindsided. I didn't see it coming. My gift was gone. My sisters were trapped. It was—"

"Bruno—just because you saw something,"

Roberto said haltingly, "that doesn't mean it has to happen, you know? Your gift isn't absolute—"

Roberto kept talking, but Bruno didn't hear him. Couldn't make out the words. He didn't want to hear what Roberto said, didn't need platitudes in the moment. He needed silence. A chance to think and try to figure out what to do next. But Roberto kept talking. Slowly, his words got softer, replaced by the *thump-thump-thump* of Bruno's feet on the dirt, then the cobblestone as he ran for home.

◎◎◎◎◎

Agustín Espinoza sniffed the bunch of flowers he held in his hands. They were freshly picked from his mother's backyard. Agustín straightened his thin frame and pushed his wiry glasses up the bridge of his nose to examine the bouquet. They were a nice mix of roses, lilies, and tulips. He'd selected them meticulously, like a painter deciding which colors to use on their canvas. He didn't want to mess this up.

He stumbled slightly as the terrain shifted from the dirt path to the cobblestone of Encanto's main square, on his way to Casita. On his way to Julieta. He'd decided late the night before, as he stared up at the ceiling, to let his feelings be known. To finally admit to Julieta, his friend and someone he cared about deeply, that his emotions were more than just companionship. He was falling for her.

It wasn't just that Julieta was beautiful, though she was. She was razor-sharp and savvy but also carried with her a strong and caring heart. Agustín had lost count of the times Julieta had come by his house with a bandeja paisa or empanadas for him to snack on as he recovered from his latest trip or fall. Agustín's mind was always in the clouds. He was always plotting and thinking and dreaming. Sometimes that didn't sync well with other things—like walking and talking. But Julieta's gift was special. Her meals could literally heal people, as they'd often helped him. He knew she cared for him, too, but still—he wasn't sure. Did she love him? he wondered.

He looked at Casita as he approached. The house loomed large for him and everyone who lived in the Encanto. It was a symbol of all they'd sacrificed to build this haven—this community that protected them and served them. Encanto provided them all with everything they could ever need. An oasis of peace and happiness that seemed almost like a fairy tale. Agustín felt a surge of gratitude.

He saw Julieta step out onto the front porch of the house and started to wave but pulled back. There was someone else approaching. A dapper-looking young man. Tall, handsome, well-kept.

Roberto.

He had seen him with Bruno earlier, but then Julieta's brother had run off. *He must've followed Bruno home*, Agustín thought.

Agustín had known for a while he was not Julieta's ideal suitor. Alma Madrigal, Julieta's stern but caring mother, had made it clear to him in as many words. Julieta deserved the best. And when you told someone who was interested in dating your daughter that she deserved the best, the implication was clear: Agustín was not the best.

Roberto approached Julieta. Agustín couldn't make out what they were saying, but he didn't need to. He saw Julieta smiling broadly. Saw Roberto take her hands playfully. Saw them hug. A lingering, familiar hug.

His heart sank.

He didn't hear the flowers hit the ground. Didn't see Julieta look up as he turned around and started the long walk back home. Didn't hear her call his name in confusion as he picked up the pace, his shoes sliding into the dusty path, covering his clothes with a fine film of dirt.

⊚⊚⊚⊚⊚

Time passed differently for Bruno. Or at least it felt that way.

In his mind, he knew it'd been a few days since he'd stormed off, leaving Roberto behind. But here, in his room, it seemed like no time at all had passed. He basked in that uncertainty—that feeling of not knowing, exactly, how long he'd been home. The shutters closed. The lights out. The only sound the murmur and buzz of the Encanto outside his tiny window. Casita felt safe, warm, secluded—but for how long? Bruno wondered. If his vision was true, the entire town could be overwhelmed by a relentless darkness. And he could feel, somehow, that it was happening soon. It would be a danger and evil he wouldn't be able to stop before it was too late.

He looked up from his seat on the floor, his eyes becoming accustomed to the darkness, even though it was midday. Bruno had to do something. Could Roberto be right? Could Bruno's own visions be wrong? They'd never been wrong before. Could Bruno try to change what he'd seen?

His thoughts were interrupted by a slight rapping sound at the door.

Bruno leapt to his feet and gently opened the door. He was not surprised to see her on the other side.

"¿Bruno, puedo pasar?" his mami asked.

He nodded. He watched as his mami's expression went from neutral to mild concern as she realized he'd been sitting in the dark alone for what felt to him like hours, but which he knew was several days.

"You've been in here for a long time," Alma said, her voice calm and soothing. Bruno knew she had been in this role before, the sedate narrator trying to pull Bruno back to her, back to the wider world. He felt a pang of guilt. "Come to the kitchen. Let me make you something and then we can sit outside and talk, okay? ¿Está bien?"

Bruno nodded as Alma turned and left. He wasn't hungry, but even he could pick up the clues she was dropping. She was worried, and when Alma was worried, she acted. She didn't sit and wait for something else to happen. She hadn't been raised that way, and neither had her children. Her family had been forged in tragedy and magic, and the entire town continued to exist because of Alma's sheer willpower. She didn't let things roll over her.

Bruno didn't remember much of those early days—the formative ones for Encanto, Casita, and their gifts. But he did understand the central role Mami played. She did it all. While everyone complained or threw in their two cents, Alma did the work and made sure the town was a functional and safe place for all its residents. She maintained the link to the magic that pulsed through the town. She was the connective tissue that kept everyone going. The town took her for granted, Bruno knew. He did, as well. But he also knew how it wore her down. There wasn't a night when Bruno came home to find his mother already asleep. First to rise, last to bed, always moving, always working.

He tried to consider that every time he spoke to her. Bruno, for all his inner grief, hated to be a bother. He wanted to be able to handle himself on his own and didn't want to be any more of a burden on his mother than his sisters were. But he couldn't deny the fact that he was troubled. That the very gift Encanto had bestowed on him was causing him great distress.

The thoughts hovered around him as he took the stairs down from his room to Casita's main foyer. He could smell something sumptuous wafting from the kitchen. Could hear Pepa humming to herself down another hallway. The house was harmonious, Bruno thought—did it really need him? Was he helping or hurting the Encanto?

"Bruno, your look is worth a million words."

Alma's comment made Bruno look up to see his mother at the foot of the stairs, gazing at her only son, a concerned smile on her face.

"Come sit with your mami, Bruno," she said, motioning to him. He did as she suggested, following her into a small parlor off the main entryway.

She pointed to a large, cozy chair near the entrance and took a seat on the small sofa across from it.

"I'm fine, Mami," Bruno said before fully sitting down. "Estoy cansado. That's all, okay?"

"¿Bruno, cómo puedes estar cansado?" she admonished gently. "You sleep until the early afternoon unless there's a reason to get out of bed. Then you wander the town like a lost boy. People are starting to talk, mijo. Tell me, is there something going on?"

He opened his mouth to respond but thought better of it. What could he say?

"Is something going on at school? Is someone bothering you?"

"No, Mami, it's . . . it's not like that."

"Then what is it?" she asked, leaning forward, her tan elbows on her knees as she peered at him with wide eyes. Bruno could see she was completely at a loss. What could he say to help her? he wondered. And would that, in turn, help him?

"Mami, do you ever feel like—well, like that thing everyone tells you is great about you, that gift is, well . . . not that?" Bruno said, struggling with each word. "I don't know how to explain it, but—you feel like that thing you're supposed to be, that everyone wants you to be—isn't what *you* want to be?"

Bruno scanned Alma's face, hoping for a flash of recognition—of acceptance—but saw a blank stare instead. In a moment, her mouth turned up slightly in a smile.

"Ay, Bruno, I don't know what you're saying. It's normal to feel weird as a teenager. I mean, look at your sisters," she said with a dry laugh, waving her hand upward as if gesturing to Julieta and Pepa upstairs. "But there's so much in life to enjoy, Bruno. So much to do. So much to give back to this town that has given us so much, too."

She didn't get it. The words seemed to burn themselves into Bruno's mind before his mother finished talking. A heavy, soggy sadness enveloped him, a weighty anchor he couldn't pull away from.

"Listen to me, mi amor," she said, placing a warm hand on his. "This is what you need to do."

She took in a deep breath, and her knowing smile became more forced.

"You have to get out more. Tienes que hacer más," she said. Bruno could tell she was sharing each word slowly, hoping they'd catch on for him.

"Spend time with your friends, run around, enjoy this life that we have. Hang out with Roberto more. He seems like a good boy, and I know he is interested in your sister. How great would it be for your best friend to marry tu hermanita, ¿eh? Try to enjoy the people around you. Don't spend all your time in your head, worrying about things that will never come to pass."

"But, Mami—"

Alma interrupted him.

"If this is about Pepa's wedding, don't worry," she said, her voice lowering to a whisper. "Your sister is over it. She is somewhere else now. She loves you very much. No te preocupes, okay? It's over now."

A simmering annoyance bubbled up in Bruno.

"I saw the rain, Mami, and it rained," he said flatly. "I didn't want to lie to anyone."

Alma let out a long, frustrated sigh.

"It's not about lying, Bruno," she said. "It's about knowing when to say anything at all. Do you understand? Who wants to hear about rain on their wedding day, mi niño? People don't like bad news. Ever. It's not the kind of thing people can process."

"But my gift—"

"Your gift is amazing. You are amazing. But you also need to learn how to use it," Alma said. "If all you do is share bad news and sad news, you will be the loneliest boy in Encanto."

Alma got up.

"I have to see what your sisters are up to," she said as Bruno also rose to his feet. She gave him a quick peck on the cheek and a tight hug. "Te quiero mucho."

Bruno waited a few moments and watched Alma leave the room. Her words echoed in his mind.

You will be the loneliest boy in Encanto.

But what if he already was?

Still, he had an idea. And he knew just how to make it work.

Maybe.

Excerpt from Julieta Madrigal's Diary

Mami wants me to decide. She has made this clear. Not expressly—Mami doesn't operate that way. But more subtly. "¿Y cuando vas a tener un novio serio?" The question is infrequent, but impactful. When will I find a boyfriend, Mami? I don't know. Why do I need one? Especially now—as I still feel that sinking, heavy feeling each time I come back to Casita. Especially when I look at Bruno and see him struggling with himself. With his gift.

I often think about how easy Pepa and I have it. Our gifts are transactional, almost. I make food, people eat it, they are healed. Pepa—depending on her mood—can affect the weather. It's an action. But Bruno can't help it. If he sees someone, he can also see what's next. Not control what's next. At least that's not how I understood his gift.

Padilla has cropped up again, too. I know Mami doesn't trust him. There's some connection between them, something that dates to the early days of Encanto. She rarely speaks of him—and when she does,

it's to warn us away. Surely she's noticed that Bruno and the old man are spending more time together.

In my heart, I don't get a sense that Francisco Padilla is a bad man. But I've been wrong before. And Bruno is innocent. Like us, his sisters, he thinks the best of others. Expects them to be honest and true in all their affairs. He's a good-hearted boy. But that's not always helpful.

Oh, diary, how I can ramble! What do you do when your entries could bore the diary you write them in?

Roberto came by. He's clearly interested in being more than friends. At the same time, I saw Agustín, and Bruno apparently turned Hernán away at the doors of Casita. It's too much. I don't have time for any of them. I don't have time for Roberto's smooth operations, Agustín's anxiety, or Hernán's ego. When I find someone I want to be with, I will let them know. No sooner, no later. I don't need to be defined by the person I'm partnered with. I am my own person.

And right now? I'm worried about my brother.

CHAPTER
NINE

Bruno bounded back up the stairs to his room, the idea burning in his mind. This was it, he figured. This was the answer.

He closed the door behind him and settled into a seated position in the middle of his room. He took a series of deep breaths. He was scared, but he couldn't be if this was going to work, he told himself. He had to be calm. He had to be open to what the gift held for him.

He had to see his own future.

Bruno had never thought to do this—hadn't understood his gift enough to even try, if he was being honest. It'd always seemed like a reactionary ability. He'd interact or engage with someone, and the vision would appear. It wasn't something Bruno activated or even tried to control. But maybe he could change that, he thought. Maybe he could cut out the randomness of it, and he could see what was in store for him.

But did he want to?

Bruno shook the doubt away. Of course he did. Encanto was a magical place. His family was wonderful. Casita was warm and welcoming. The future had to be bright. His future would be bright.

So why were his hands shaking?

Bruno swallowed hard and closed his eyes.

Nothing. Only the darkness of his own eyelids, the sound of wind chimes, and the bustle of Encanto outside.

He took another deep breath, waiting patiently. He'd never tried to will a vision into being, so he wasn't sure how long it might take. Usually Bruno's gift was like a primal, instinctive reflex.

He was about to open his eyes when he saw it: the flickering of a green light in the darkness of his own mind, a potent glow that grew to consume everything around him. But the light seemed safe— familiar. Bruno waited. Then another image formed, of Casita—a large family dinner, his mother, Alma, at the head of the table full of guests. And somehow, Bruno just knew who they were. Family. He saw Julieta, older, married to a man whose face he could not make out. Bruno saw her children, looking at her with loving eyes and admiration. He saw Pepa and Félix. He saw neighbors and friends. He could smell the food spread out before them—arroz con pollo, dulce de leche for dessert, an array of appetizers the kids were greedily grabbing. Bruno waited patiently as the camera of his mind wound down and around the table, lingering on each guest, until finally, he could wait no more.

Where was he?

Where was Bruno?

As if understanding his question, the vision floated up and away from the boisterous and fun meal, beyond Casita's dining room to another part of the house, through a dark, cavernous crawl space that Bruno knew was a secret to everyone in the vision—everyone but him. He could feel the dirt under his fingertips and smell the musty air. He could hear the skittering of rats scurrying around and in front of him. A chill washed over him, like he was tied to a chair being forced to watch something terrifying, except he knew what it was. And he knew how it was supposed to end.

Bruno swallowed hard as the vision continued to unfurl, the world around him gone, replaced by this other world, similar yet so different. The tunnel grew narrower and darker until a slight shaft of light shone through. Then Bruno saw it. He saw the figure, huddled in a corner, mumbling sounds emanating from it. Bruno could make out a tattered green hood cloaking the figure. The silhouettes of rats on the figure's shoulders. Bruno knew what he was seeing, knew without knowing—and in his heart, he felt it. This was no stranger.

He knew before the figure pulled the hood back to reveal Bruno himself, but older—the facial hair, the dark bags under his eyes, the tousled and oily hair, the energetic glow of his pupils. It was still Bruno. But what had he become? Who was this Bruno, and what had he seen to make him this way?

Why had he decided to hide himself inside the walls of his own home?

Before Bruno could think it over in more detail, the vision seemed to notice him—something that

Bruno had never experienced before. The visions had always been just that—peeks into futures and unchangeable moments. Like watching a painting coming together or listening to a story in your mind. It existed on its own plane, apart from the reality Bruno resided in. But this was different. This was new. And as Bruno looked into his own, older eyes, he felt himself become unmoored, as if he were floating in deep water, unable to move to safety.

And then his alter ego spoke. Or did he? Bruno couldn't be sure if he was seeing himself speak or if he was imagining what this version of Bruno would say.

"This is what you have to look forward to, Bruno," he thought he heard his alternate self say, a snide grin on his face—a knowing, defeated look. "No one wants to hear you. No one wants to know what the future holds if it's like this. You'll be shamed and shunned for your gift, and the only people you love, your family, won't even care."

The vision crashed into darkness, disappearing into a million sharp pieces as Bruno backed away, his body sliding across the floor, his pulse racing. He could feel the room—his room—closing in on him. He could still hear the words—echoing in his mind—as he backpedaled out of it. As he sped down the stairs.

As he ran outside screaming.

But what Bruno didn't hear—what he chose to ignore as he ran—could have changed much of what was to come. He could've seen his older self smiling gently. He could've seen that Bruno turn to him, eyes watering, a soft smile on his face. He could've heard the words that might have made a difference and spared him so much pain.

CHAPTER
TEN

I see him run out. I hear Bruno screaming in fear.

His eyes are wide, as if he's seen a ghost. But I know it's not a ghost. It's something else. Something even more frightening.

In the quiet that follows, I step closer to the house—out of the view of his mother, his sisters, and anyone else. I've been around Encanto long enough to know where to step. How to hide my movements. How to fit in and be part of the crowd. I know where Bruno will run, too. To his friend. To hope. To some kind of absolution. Anything that can prevent him from coming to terms with the reality that what he saw, the darkness he peered into, will come to pass. Sooner than he could ever imagine.

I hear chimes in the distance. I hear muffled

voices. But it's what I see that matters most. I see the jagged line forming at the bottom of Casita. A tiny, infinitesimal crack. A broken part. A sign of disruption.

Seeing that, I know. In my heart, I know what's to come.

I've been watching him. Waiting for this moment. And now it's almost upon us.

The complete and utter destruction of Casita. Of the selfish, egotistical people inside and everything that holds Encanto together—the magic, the trust, the family. It all ends soon, and I will have a front-row seat to its destruction.

I laugh. A low, hearty laugh. The kind of laugh that isn't about humor—but about release, and about something else. Something deeper and darker and so much more flavorful.

It's about revenge.

CHAPTER
ELEVEN

Bruno ran. He felt the wind slapping his face, felt his feet slapping the cobblestone—thrumming with each hurried step. Bruno felt the fear envelop him, felt the heat of the run and of his panic cover every inch of him.

He had never been so scared.

The thought slammed into him as he pivoted around the town square, sidestepping and dodging children, food stands, neighbors, and strangers. All reacting in the same way—in surprise. Why was Bruno running? Where was Alma Madrigal's strange son off to? He didn't know, either. Might never know. He didn't want to stop running. Because stopping would mean coming to terms with what he'd seen.

Coming to terms with himself. With his own darkness. With his own future.

But he didn't have to stop himself. Someone else did it for him.

Bruno didn't see the hand stretched out in front of him until it was too late, and his body slammed into the figure it belonged to. He pulled back, trying to minimize the damage, but fell to the ground. He looked up to see a tall, lanky figure. He recognized him immediately.

Francisco Padilla reached down—his hand extended to Bruno, who looked up—his expression a mix of surprise and shame. Bruno took Padilla's hand and tried to dust himself off as he got to his feet. He'd never thought Padilla, of all people, would see him like this—terrified and unhinged—but so be it, Bruno thought. What could he do?

"¿Bruno, adónde corres, mijo?" Padilla asked, placing a hand on Bruno's shoulder. "Are you running a race?"

Bruno shook his head slightly. He was still catching his breath, but even then, he wasn't sure he'd have a concrete answer for the older man who stood next to him. Not anything he'd be able to say with a straight face, even to Padilla, someone Bruno knew and trusted. That put Padilla in very select company.

Though the Encanto was a warm, welcoming place, there were still outcasts. People who lived on the margins of the town—who were part of the environment but not necessarily embraced by all. Bruno felt himself inching further into that category, but he knew Padilla was already a longtime resident. Older, at least fifteen years or so ahead of Alma, Bruno's mother, Padilla had a long scraggly gray beard and often wandered Encanto in a tattered dark green ruana, his face and features masked. His reasons were simple enough—it was hot, and he preferred to be under permanent shade. Whispers about Padilla were incessant—that he was a wizard of some kind, that he practiced the dark arts, that he had murdered his own family—and though Bruno didn't believe any, they were enough to deter people, like his own mother, from engaging with or trusting him too much. Children were warned away. Adults crossed the street when they saw Padilla walking toward them. Vendors sold him fruit and food hastily for fear of losing the line of customers behind him. Francisco Padilla was so much more than the rumors, though, Bruno knew. He was a kind and thoughtful man—albeit a mysterious one. Bruno knew little about Padilla's past, his perspectives on Encanto and the people in it, or where he hung his hat. But Bruno did know one thing: Padilla was kind to him and seemed to care about Bruno's struggles in a genuine, deep way that was lacking in almost every other interaction the young man had in town, or even with his family. Aside from Roberto, Padilla was his only friend, and Bruno treasured that.

He did not, however, feel great about seeing him now—at what felt like his lowest point in quite some time.

"No, nada, I'm fine," Bruno said, still out of breath. Padilla draped his arm over Bruno's shoulders and pulled him off the street toward a nearby bench. They took a seat together, Padilla's eyes expectant, even under the dark hood that had become his defining look.

"You're not fine," Padilla said with a soft shake of his head. "Don't tell me that. Something happened. You're a deeply feeling young man, Bruno. You wear your heart on your sleeve. I see it. You're scared and worried. Why? Can I help you? Dime algo."

Bruno took in a sharp breath. He was scared;

Padilla was right. But what could he say to this man about what he'd seen? What he'd felt?

"I'm just . . . I'm not feeling great," Bruno said, unable to meet Padilla's eyes. "It feels like there's a lot going on and I can't control it—I have no power to, I dunno, change what's coming."

Bruno kept his eyes on his hands but heard Padilla clear his throat, then speak in a soft, calm voice.

"Claro, Bruno, that's a totally normal feeling," Padilla said. He motioned toward Bruno. "Get up. Let's walk. Let's get our blood pumping and brain working, eh?"

Bruno did as he was told and followed a half step behind the older man as they wound down one of the many side streets that crisscrossed Encanto. It was an alley, the back side of a residential stretch. Bruno could hear windows closing and the skittering of footsteps as people left their balconies upon seeing Padilla and Bruno coming their way. But he ignored it, the same way Padilla did, though with perhaps less grace.

"Does this have to do with your gift?" Padilla

said, still a few paces ahead, looking toward the end of the short alley. "Because I have to imagine that weighs on you a lot, Bruno."

Bruno didn't respond. He wasn't sure he wanted to talk about this, but it did help to share, no? To connect?

"You're growing up, Bruno," Padilla continued. "You're no longer a kid. You're seeing the bad and the good. The problem is, you have a way to see the bad and the good that's about to happen—or at least a version of it. If there's one thing I've learned over the years, mijo, it's that people often cannot handle the truth. They don't like it. And I don't mean harsh, cruel truths—though those are hard to swallow. I just mean reality. Science. Facts. Truth. They want to create their own narratives. Things that soothe their worldview and make them feel safe. But we live in an unsafe world, Bruno. We live in a place of conflict and change and stress. The best way to approach that is with eyes open—and with hope. With an understanding that nothing is set in stone until it happens, and even then, even when something bad happens, we must believe it's part of a greater plan for us. That's what I hope you'll believe, too."

Bruno had caught up with Padilla and found himself walking next to the cloaked man.

"So . . . you don't think the future is written?"

Padilla turned to look at Bruno, an incredulous expression on his face.

"Do you?"

Bruno furrowed his brow.

"I'm—well, I dunno," he said. "I'm not sure. When I see something—when I feel my gift, it happens."

"I'm sure it does," Padilla said with a knowing nod. "But do you think it happens because it was meant to be—or because you saw it and somehow willed it to happen?"

A wave of dizziness hit Bruno, as if he'd just been spun off the edge of a lake or wide pool and was spiraling down into the water. He stopped walking and tried to get ahold of himself.

"Bruno, are you all right?" Padilla asked. But his voice sounded distant, muted.

It took a few moments for Bruno to speak, but his words seemed to hang between him and his old friend like a scroll unspooled.

"If I can control these things, if I can somehow will them to be, then I can also do the opposite," he said. "I don't have to be locked into what I see. Especially if there's time to change it. My future isn't written. I'm not locked into someone else's plan or script. I'm my own person."

Bruno looked up at Padilla.

"Right?"

Padilla opened his mouth to respond, but Bruno was already gone. He looked down the alley and watched the young man speeding toward some unknown destination.

And Francisco Padilla smiled.

CHAPTER
TWELVE

The plan came together quickly.

Bruno saw the pieces floating in front of his face as he ran back toward the town square. Saw them clicking into place as he slowed down and began to pace in front of Casita. Could it work? he wondered. He wasn't sure. But he did know one thing: he was going to change the future. The vision of a dark cloud looming over Encanto could not come to pass. Even just thinking about it—about the villagers running around, lost and confused—gave Bruno pause. He wouldn't allow it. He wasn't going to be held hostage by his visions. He was not going to be sentenced to life as a pariah.

A small voice cut through the noise, from the back of his mind. A questioning thought that, at first, Bruno just wanted to ignore. But it rose up anyway.

Was that what Francisco Padilla meant? Was it about control—or about finding your place in the greater plan?

Bruno shook his head. No, it wasn't either. It wasn't about control—though Bruno did have it. He could decide what to do, and he would use his gift—his power—to ensure that he avoided the traumatic vision he'd witnessed in his own room. He couldn't allow himself to become that . . . that creature. That monster. He wouldn't accept it. If it meant subverting his own gift, then so be it. He would sacrifice this wondrous ability if it meant he could be happy—at peace.

"Peso for your thoughts, hermano?"

It was Julieta, lugging a bag of groceries and heading toward Casita. She had a slight smile on her face—the look of someone who'd been daydreaming and found themselves pulled out of the fantasy by reality. The reality being her brother, wandering the streets of the town deep in thought.

"Hola, trilliza," Bruno said, giving his triplet a warm hug. "No change to spare, sadly. Just trying to figure some stuff out."

"Aren't we all," she said, handing him the bag.

"Help your overworked sister lug some vegetales to Mami?"

Bruno nodded, and they walked toward Casita.

"What's on your mind, then?" Bruno asked.

Julieta shrugged.

"Ay, it's nothing, but I'm kind of fed up," she said, her voice sounding strained. "I love Mami, of course. Love everyone in our house. But sometimes I just wish she'd—I dunno. This sounds terrible, Dios. I wish she'd just let me be, ¿tú sabes? Let me decide for myself."

"Is this about Pepa?" Bruno asked.

"Sort of, but not directly," Julieta said. "I'm happy for her. I love Félix. But just because she got married doesn't mean we have to run and do the same, right? Doesn't she ask you about it?"

Bruno laughed.

"I think she's just worried about me, period. She'd love for me to get married to someone—anyone," he said. They both chuckled. "I think you're feeling it more because you're a girl, which is a problem in its own way."

"Sure is, sib," Julieta said. "I just don't feel the same pressure. When I meet someone—if I meet someone—I will know. Maybe right away. Maybe over time. But I swear, if I start scrambling to find Señor Perfecto, I will never find him. The future is not—"

"Written in stone," Bruno finished. They looked at each other, as if both were awakening from the same dream. "Yeah, I agree. Totally. I . . ."

Bruno struggled with the words. He could see his sister's expectant gaze, waiting for him to say more—to finally reveal himself to her. But he couldn't. There was still more to do. He had so much work to do.

"Look, hermanita, I have to go, okay? But let's talk more about this, huh? I think—well, I think you're on to something."

Julieta grabbed his arm. She was not accustomed to people wandering away from her.

"Bruno, what on earth are you talking about?"

Bruno pulled away before turning to face his sister, a knowing smile on his face.

"You'll see."

☯☯☯☯☯

Encanto needed a hero. And Bruno needed to be that hero.

That was the realization that kept ringing in Bruno's mind as he paced around his room. It was the only way, he thought, to prevent the dark future he'd witnessed. To save not only himself but Encanto, as well.

But how could he do that?

The way things stood now, everyone in the town looked to Bruno with a wary eye. They were either hesitant to engage with him or downright scared, and that all but ensured the solitary existence that would lead him to actualize the vision. The crawl spaces. The rats. The loneliness.

Bruno shook his head. No. He wouldn't allow that.

But *whom* could he be more like? What did a hero do? And whom would the townspeople want to rally around?

He heard a slight rapping on his door.

"Come in," he said.

Before he'd finished, his door creaked open and Roberto stepped in, a bright smile on his face.

"Your mami says you've been holed up in here

por mucho de la semana, Bruno," Roberto said, plopping down on Bruno's small bed. He looked flushed and happy, cheerful. Roberto scanned the clothes strewn around the room and piled on the floor. "You really need some new clothes, Bruno."

He ignored the comment. Roberto had been campaigning against Bruno's lack of fashion sense for almost as long as Bruno had known him. Bruno realized he'd never seen his friend upset, had never seen him frown, really. How did he live such a life? Bruno wondered. Without a care in the world? Was it possible?

"I've just had a lot on my mind," Bruno said, still pacing around the room. "I'm trying to figure something—figure myself out."

Roberto nodded, as if he'd been spending time in Bruno's head.

"You're stressed out. I can see it. Your sister mentioned it, too."

Bruno bristled at the idea of Julieta talking about him behind his back. But he also understood. Bruno *had* been acting on edge. She was worried about him. Bruno appreciated that. But he also would prefer to work out his problems on his own.

"Julieta doesn't know what's going on," Bruno snapped, instantly regretting his tone.

"She's just looking out for you," Roberto said with a shrug. "Your mom seems concerned, too. She told me she saw you—saw you talking to that old man, Padilla, today."

Bruno stiffened. He knew Alma Madrigal was wary of Francisco Padilla. Had been since Bruno could remember. She'd tried to remain neutral when discussing him with Bruno, but he'd heard her opinion secondhand. She considered him a trickster and a fraud, a man who relied on sleight of hand and vague phrases to lull people into believing his ideas. She had confided in Julieta more than once that she thought the cloaked man was a bad influence on Bruno in particular.

"So what if I was?" Bruno said, his tone softer but his words still sharp. "He's my friend."

"Yeah? You seem to be his only amigo," Roberto said, motioning for Bruno to sit next to him. Bruno did. "I just worry about you sometimes, bro. You seem troubled. I just want to help you."

Bruno looked into his friend's eyes and felt a pang of guilt for being so curt with Roberto. Like

Padilla, Roberto was in select company—one of the few people in Encanto who was friends with Bruno and tolerated him, not because they had to or because they were related to him. It should mean something, Bruno thought.

He placed a hand on his friend's shoulder.

"I appreciate it," Bruno said. "I know I worry everyone sometimes."

"Sometimes?" Roberto responded with a laugh. "You're a giant mystery to your family."

Bruno looked down at his hands.

"I need to change myself," he said, as much to himself as to Roberto, vocalizing the realization he'd had with Padilla a few hours before.

"What?"

"Remember that vision I told you about?" Bruno asked, staring across his cramped room, the light of the small window above his bed cutting through the dusty air. "I saw myself. A future version of me. And . . . and it scared me."

Roberto stood up in surprise.

"Wait, what? Are you telling me you took your own—you checked your own future? Can you even do that?" Roberto asked.

Bruno shrugged.

"I did, so I can, and what I saw freaked me out," Bruno said. "I must do whatever I can to stop that from coming true. I have to save myself. And the Encanto."

"The Encanto . . ." Roberto repeated.

Bruno nodded quickly.

"Yes, yes, when I saw . . . a kind of future for the village," Bruno said, repeating what he'd told his friend days ago. "Someone . . . something had betrayed us all. Left us open to a darkness creeping in. Like a thick gray cloud. Something that was going to hurt everything we'd built. And I can't let that be."

Roberto crouched down in front of Bruno, looking up at his friend.

"Does seeing a vision guarantee it's true, though?" Roberto asked. "What can I do to help?"

Bruno let out a dry laugh.

"Remember that idea you had the other day about changing everything?"

CHAPTER
THIRTEEN

Here goes nada, Bruno thought as he walked out of the house.

The shiny silk shirt Roberto had loaned him felt slimy and awkward on his thin frame. The tight black pants were uncomfortable on his legs. He didn't even want to think about what the loafers were doing to his wide feet. But he looked good. Most important, he looked different. The air whipped past him, glancing off his bare neck, now visible with his hair up in a tidy bun. Bruno felt the stares the second he took a few paces toward the town square. Double takes, whispers of "¿Es Bruno Madrigal?" and a few chuckles of discomfort. But he fought the urge to turn and run, to toss the uncomfortable clothes into his closet and hide in his dark room. He wasn't doing this just for the sake of fashion. He was doing it to save himself, and his friends and family. He had no choice, he rationalized.

The conversation with Roberto had been helpful. His friend had guided Bruno through his general thought—that he had to be different somehow—to something workable. Bruno had to become someone else, to change himself and become more of a positive force in the town. Jovial, cheerful, friendly, outspoken, and most important, happy.

Roberto pointed to people like the boisterous and loud Félix, who'd managed to woo Bruno's own sister Pepa. Or his classmate Carlos, who seemed to be the star of everything he participated in— whether it was the school play or any given sport. Bruno needed to strive for that, Roberto said. He had to change how people saw him, and that might change how they approached him. Roberto had even suggested Bruno change his clothes—try to be more fashionable.

So far, though, Bruno thought—it wasn't working. He was just getting strange looks and the same wide berth he'd always gotten when walking around the town. A long, defeated sigh formed in his lungs, but he stopped himself. No, the new Bruno wouldn't do that. He'd smile and laugh it off. So that was what Bruno did.

"Hey, lookin' good, Bruno."

It was Annalise, one of his classmates. She gave him a radiant, toothy smile. Bruno had to think for a second before responding in kind. He expected that to be it. They'd move away from each other, and he'd spend a few days mulling over what he'd done wrong. Instead, she stepped toward him.

"Is that a new shirt? There's something— I dunno—different about you." She seemed to be sizing him up, not in a predatory way but with admiration—like someone walking by a bright flower or classical statue they'd missed before. "It's cool. I like it."

Bruno straightened up, not out of fear but something else. Something weird.

Was this . . . *pride*?

"Uh, yeah, I'm trying a new look out."

"Well, it works," Annalise said with a nod before turning toward one of the main roads, which led to a more residential stretch of Encanto.

Bruno started to respond but couldn't formulate anything. He was stuck. Could this idea—this sloppy, unrefined, and confusing idea—really be working?

He took a deep breath and kept walking.

Maybe there was something to this, he thought as he sauntered along the edges of the main food market. He could see vendors of all kinds selling their finest—fruits, meats, vegetables, prepared meals, spices. The Encanto market was a sensory thrill ride, and one of Bruno's favorite parts of the town. It was a peek into the wider world, and it warmed his heart (and mouth, and stomach) to sample the various delicacies being sold. But lately, even the market had felt distant to him—a place where he'd be judged just for being there. Frightened looks. Awkward glances. He braced for it, even now. But somehow, this walk felt different. It was almost as if everyone had seen his interaction with Annalise. Had witnessed some kind of transformation. This new, confident Bruno had erased the boy who had been there before.

Maybe that was okay, Bruno thought.

Perhaps the trick here was to not only pretend to be confident, jolly, and smooth but to forget who he was before? To ignore the person he was inside and become the act itself?

He got a bitter taste in his mouth as the thought crystallized in his mind. Something seemed off about it. But you couldn't argue with results, could you?

"Oye, Bruno—¿y tus hermanitas, cómo están?"

It was Señor Cruz, the butcher. His tent was draped with the finest pieces of meat, cut in every which way. The line of people waiting for their chance to get the best cuts in town wove around the tent and down the block. But Cruz was leaning over his counter and looking at Bruno.

"Están bien, Señor Cruz," Bruno said, trying to keep his voice deep—confident. Direct. It seemed to be working. The butcher was nodding in approval. "Tú sabes."

The last two words were shared with a knowing shrug, as if Cruz and Bruno were old pals swapping stories from long ago. But Bruno had no idea what he was suggesting Cruz knew. Cruz probably didn't, either. But Bruno also realized there was some ceremony here—some kind of dance he'd never engaged in. A verbal tennis match that felt awkward to Bruno but also sounded so very common.

Was this small talk? he thought.

The butcher let out a long, boisterous laugh, pointing a finger at Bruno playfully as the younger man walked farther into the market's twisting alleys and walkways. Bruno waved in response. He could still hear Cruz's laughter as he continued on his way.

It all seemed to be working, Bruno thought—but now what? Would Bruno just get used to this new way of life—this new self? Could he? He had to admit, it felt weird. Unnatural. But the results spoke for themselves. Already, just after interacting with Annalise and the butcher, Cruz, he could see the other villagers looking at the new version of Bruno with something else on their faces . . . something warmer. A kindness and openness that had seemed forever lost to Bruno. He liked it. If he was being honest, he craved it.

He felt a slight tap on his shoulder. He spun around. It was an older woman, one he'd seen a few times over the years. Señora Anta, a seamstress who lived on the edge of town. She'd always been friendly to Bruno and his sisters. Had even visited the house from time to time to have cafecito with his mami. She looked shaken, though, out of sorts. Bruno started to reach for her, but then she spoke.

"Bruno . . . perdón, pero . . . necesito tu ayuda," she said sheepishly. Bruno could tell that this request for help was hard for the older woman, who had always struck Bruno as regal and refined.

"Claro, Señora Anta, whatever you want," Bruno said with an eager nod. And he meant it. This was what he desired. He needed the villagers to recognize and appreciate him—but even if it meant they were appreciating another, unrealistic version of Bruno? That was still to be determined.

She reached out and clutched Bruno's hands in hers. They were well-worn and clammy. Bruno looked into her eyes and saw a panic and desperation that was new to him. It made his heart sink.

"Bruno, it's . . . it's my husband, Julio," she said haltingly. "He's been ill—sleeping all day, lethargic, feverish. It has gone on for so many days now. El Doctor Lobo says there's nothing else he can do. That it is up to God. But tu mami—she has told me over and over about your gift, about what you can see. Can you help me, Bruno? Can you tell me what the future is for my Julio?"

Bruno pulled back slightly, but Señora Anta held firm, her eyes locked on his.

"Bueno, no sé. I can sometimes see—"

"No, mijo, your mami says you have the gift," she continued. "That it came to you—after your fifth birthday. You can see the future. You can tell me if my Julio will be okay. Can you look, please? I'll give you anything. Everything I have, just to know he will be okay."

Bruno wanted to reply, but he couldn't. She was sobbing now, her head buried in his new shirt, her body shaking softly. He wrapped his arms around her, patting her shoulder gently in the way he thought he should, but was unable to truly under-stand what was happening.

What do I do? he wondered. He wanted to help. He wanted to be present for this woman and for his fellow villagers. He didn't want to be shunned or ignored. He wanted to be a hero.

And didn't heroes give people hope?

He wasn't sure what he'd see if he attempted

to channel his power. He feared he would see the worst—Julio Anta shivering on his bed, near death, the priest saying the last rites. So why torment this woman with that? he thought as he listened to Señora Anta's muted sobs. Why make her struggle even worse than it already was?

He took a deep breath and spoke words he would regret for the rest of his life.

"I see him, Señora. I see him stepping out of bed—a wide smile on his face," Bruno said, each word a chore to let escape his mouth, each moment sending a shock of pain and shame through him. He didn't see this, in fact. He saw something else. Something he couldn't bring himself to share. He saw Julio, sitting on the edge of his bed—coughing violently, his body lurching over. Was he better? Perhaps. But there was no way for Bruno to be sure— and he knew this wasn't what she wanted to hear from him now. "I see him standing tall. Looking healthy. I see him running with his children in the yard. I see him laughing like before."

She pulled back from Bruno, her face wet with tears but a wide smile on her face, her mouth open in complete surprise.

"You do? My Julio will live? He will be okay?"

Bruno couldn't speak anymore. Instead, he just nodded. She didn't ask for anything else. She'd already turned around, yelling with joy, almost skipping back toward her house.

He'd done it. Instead of bringing fear and anger to someone he shared his visions with, he'd done the opposite. He'd given her hope. Even joy.

Wasn't that worth something, even if it lasted only for a short time? he mused.

Perhaps. But if that was the case . . . why did he feel so *bad*?

PART II
AVOIDING THE MIRACLE

CHAPTER
FOURTEEN

The line wrapped around the block, starting at the door to Casita.

It had grown slowly after he'd shared his vision with Señora Anta, starting with a few people and mushrooming into something Bruno could scarcely believe.

Bruno watched as Alma shook her head with great concern.

"Es que no entiendo," she muttered to herself. "Why, Bruno, suddenly—are these people here? Waiting to talk to you?"

Bruno shrugged as he looked through Casita's main doorway. The line consisted of people from every part of the village: friends, acquaintances, teachers, vendors, children, the elderly, some with pets, even. All there to listen to Bruno. To see if he might have a moment to look into their future and assure them that, yes, everything would be fine.

For Bruno, the experience had been mixed. Like what he'd told Señora Anta, some of the "visions" Bruno shared had been invented out of whole cloth—things he thought people wanted to hear. Some had been real byproducts of his gift—things he saw the usual way, the burden lifted when what he saw in his mind was actual good news. It felt good to Bruno, reassuring him that his choice had been the right one. That he was actually doing something positive for the people who lived here.

It had started the week before, Bruno recalled. Señora Anta had wasted no time spreading the word—Bruno Madrigal could see the future, and, boy, was the future bright. Suddenly, Bruno couldn't walk anywhere without being stopped. People were asking at every opportunity. Could he tell them what would happen? Would they get this job? Would they fix their house? Would their child start sleeping well? Would their elderly parents' health improve? Would their prayers be answered? It had been too much for Bruno to handle, even under the guise of his new jovial persona. He wanted to run. To hide. To close the doors of his room and escape into the crawl spaces that existed under and around Casita. The areas he'd wandered so many times. Well, before the vision. Before he'd seen a future where he lived in those spaces—where he'd become a true outcast, from not only his family but the entire world. He wanted to avoid that dark vision, he knew. But at what cost?

He'd managed to dodge most of the requests—sequestering himself in Casita as best he could—but that had ended that morning, when Alma Madrigal stepped out onto the porch of Casita to discover half the village impatiently waiting for her son to come out and have an audience with each of them.

"Bruno, what have you done?" Alma asked, her voice hushed and stern.

His defenses went up immediately. They mixed with his already ample amounts of shame and fear to create something new, and more toxic.

"Nothing, Mami. I'm just using my gift to help people. Isn't that what you wanted me to do?" he snapped.

His mother's eyebrows popped up in surprise. Bruno had never spoken to her in this way. Not many people had. Alma Madrigal was the matriarch of the family and commanded respect from not only her children but the town. She'd saved them all, and thanks to the magical gift that had sprung up after the death of her husband, she had created something new and beautiful out of tragedy. She had suffered her share of loss. She had led them through the fire and built Encanto from nothing.

No one spoke to her like this.

"Bruno, cuida como me hablas," she said with a slight tilt of her head. Then she spun around slowly and walked up to the house's second floor. He didn't need to hear the door slam to know she was upset.

Bruno could feel his entire body tensing up. Could feel the wave of anxiety crashing down on him. But he fought back. He couldn't let himself revert to old behaviors, to ancient fears that made him what he'd been before—a strange resident of Encanto his neighbors feared and avoided. *Look at them now*, he thought as he peeked out the door again. They all wanted to see him. Wanted to spend time with him. He was helping.

He heard skittering footsteps and Julieta's sharp intake of breath. She was beside him in seconds.

"Have you lost your mind?" she asked, her hands on his shoulders as if trying to assess the damage, or get through to an alien who'd just landed on the Earth's surface.

"What?"

" 'What?' Bruno, you just snapped at Mami in the worst way possible. I'm surprised you're still alive, much less in this house," she said. "What's going on with you, hermanito?"

Bruno pulled away from his sister's grasp.

"Nothing is going on with me," he said, his tone sharper than he'd hoped. He wanted to apologize, to help Julieta understand in a calm, loving way—but wasn't that what had gotten him in this predicament in the first place? Appeasing and apologizing? Being himself? "I don't know why people keep asking me that."

Julieta scoffed.

"Bruno, it's obvious—I mean, look at you," she said, waving her arm in his direction. "You're dressing different, acting like some kind of prince, and, well, now this."

Julieta spun toward the door, moving her chin at the line of people formed outside their house.

"These people are here for you, Bruno," she said, looking at him again. "Do you have any idea why? Can you explain it to me? Because they were not here last week. Or the week before. And the only thing that's changed—is you."

Bruno's face grew hot. He wanted to talk to his sister. Explain to her all that he was feeling. But no one had ever listened before. Why would they start now? They'd always treated Bruno like the stranger—the weird child. The one they had to apologize for because he didn't pick up on the social cues, didn't laugh at the jokes at the right time or understand what certain things meant. Oh, and his gift? That was something else. The visions hid him as much as people avoided him, knowing that his visions were a roll of the dice. They might be good, but there was an equal chance they'd be bad. Who wanted to know that bad things were coming? No one, Bruno had realized. And so he'd become different. Why couldn't his own family understand that?

"So what if I have changed?" Bruno said with a careless shrug. The new Bruno wouldn't sweat this exchange, he reasoned. And he was going to act the part. It was the only way to prevent that future, and to stay part of the Encanto. "I'm just trying to help people, Julieta. I'm trying to tell them that things will be okay, that there's hope. Is that so bad?"

"It is if you're lying," Julieta said, her voice low. "It's not good for anyone. It's certainly not good for Casita. Or for Encanto. Our gifts were not meant to be used—"

"And suddenly you're an expert on Casita and our gifts?" Bruno scoffed as he sidestepped Julieta. "Suddenly you know what's best for me? Where were you when I needed you to listen? When no one wanted to talk to me, huh? Nowhere."

He felt Julieta's hand on his shoulder, but he shrugged it off.

"Bruno . . ."

"Leave me be for now, hermana," he said, his voice low and stern. It was almost like someone else was talking, using his mouth and body. And wasn't that true? Bruno needed to become another person to do some real good and to save himself, right?

He didn't watch, but he heard Julieta leave the foyer, her steps hurried and frantic. He thought he heard her sob, but he couldn't dwell on that. He had work to do.

He was someone else now. And he wanted to give the people of Encanto what they wanted: good news. Something to be grateful for. Something to cling to. He was merely giving them what they needed to get by. Life was so dark and stressful most of the time. What harm would a little good news bring?

And so what if it meant turning his back on his actual gift? His "new" visions weren't necessarily wrong; he'd just tell people what he thought they wanted to hear and let them leave his presence joyous and free, the bad news swept away by his gift and the magic that held the town together.

It was harmless.

Right?

He walked outside and stood in the sunlight bathing the front steps. He could feel everyone's eyes on him. He smiled, that polished pretend smile he'd practiced in front of the mirror for hours.

Then he motioned for the first person to step inside.

CHAPTER
FIFTEEN

"Pero what's happening, Bruno?"

The words seemed to bounce off the interior walls of Casita, lingering over Bruno like a small storm cloud. It made sense. They came from Pepa.

Bruno had snuck down for a quick snack, hoping to make it back to his room with little interference. At worst, he'd expected to run into Julieta. Maybe Mami. Pepa had not even been on his radar.

Bruno loved his twin sisters, equally and with all his heart—but he would be lying if he didn't admit he'd been avoiding Pepa. Ever since her wedding, he'd taken special care around her, tiptoeing past her as if she were a live explosive. In some ways, she was. She could be quick to anger, Bruno thought—and he wasn't up for an argument. Especially about something he couldn't change.

But it was something he could prevent from happening again.

"Hola, Pepa," Bruno said, the flimsy sandwich flopping on the plate he'd grabbed from the cupboard. He waited for Pepa to speak again. She took a hesitant step into the kitchen, her eyes on him.

"Mami tells me you've been holding court, hermanito," she said. "Telling everyone in town their prophecies. Is that true?"

Bruno swallowed hard. This was the conversation he'd been dreading. Not with Mami or Julieta—he could brace for them. But Pepa—she had experienced the dark side of Bruno's gift, even if Bruno had tried to sidestep it. He had seen a vision of rain when he saw Pepa that day—had even noticed the storm clouds forming above her head—but he realized his mistake almost immediately after mentioning the vision, backtracking and trying to play it off. It hadn't worked. Pepa knew him too well and understood that her brother didn't filter what he said. Even if Bruno had just been making a joke, it had represented what he'd *seen* coming. That was enough for Pepa, and Pepa was hard to dissuade when she believed something firmly.

"I'm trying to help people," Bruno said dryly.

Pepa crossed her arms and tilted her head as if to say, *Come on now, Bruno.*

"It's true," Bruno said, trying to keep his words light.

He just wanted to leave. A great shame washed over him. He was reminded of how he'd felt on her wedding day—the rain pouring down on him, her angry, shocked face burned into his memory like a branding iron. He was trying so hard now, he thought, to use his gift for good—to change how he was perceived by the people of his village. Why had she chosen this moment to corner him?

Pepa took another step forward and placed a hand softly on Bruno's arm. He fought the urge to pull back.

"You've been avoiding me, hermanito," she said, trying to meet his eyes.

Bruno didn't respond. There was nothing to add to the truth.

"Why?" Pepa asked. "Is your sister that scary to you?"

She is, Bruno thought, his mind flashing back to her expression. That anger. That rage.

"I didn't mean to hurt you, Pepa," Bruno said, looking down at his sandwich, unable to meet her eyes. "I want my gift to be helpful to people. Not . . . not make them mad. Or ruin their lives."

Pepa let out a long sigh.

"Bruno, your words have power. You must know that now," she said, still trying to meet his eyes. "When you walked up to me—on my wedding day— and said it looked like rain, how was I supposed to take it? How would you have interpreted it?"

Bruno looked away, looked out of the kitchen, to the world outside—to an escape from this conversation.

A slight rumble of thunder. Bruno looked at Pepa and saw a familiar tiny gray cloud above her head.

"I'm trying to be patient. I'm trying to move past what happened, Bruno," she said, and Bruno knew it was true. She was straining for calm in her voice, her actions—but if she were really over it, she wouldn't have to strain, he mused. "But I also don't want to see it happen to anyone else."

"You don't seem over it, no matter what people

tell me," Bruno said, stepping away, leaving the plate of food behind. He backpedaled, eyes still on his sister. "You're still mad about the wedding— I know it. But it wasn't my fault."

Pepa scoffed, incredulous.

"Por favor, Bruno, let's be serious—you weren't just joking," Pepa said, following him. "Dijiste lo que dijiste—you had a vision of rain, you said as much, and by saying it, you actualized it. It's time to move on, okay?"

"Is it?" Bruno asked, finally looking at Pepa, eyebrows raised as if to say, *Who's lying now?*

"What does that mean?"

"You think I ruined your wedding," Bruno said. "I'd never do that."

Pepa shook her head, looking down at her hands, which were wrapping and unwrapping from each other, a nervous habit.

"Bruno," she said, "I was upset. I never said you did it with malice, hermanito. You must know that."

Bruno was choking up. He knew he should stay and talk this through, but he wasn't sure he could handle it. He didn't want to say anything he would regret.

"I have to go," Bruno said. "I'm going to sit with more people. I'm going to show them that their futures here are good. Positive. Happy."

Pepa shook her head.

"But what if they're not?"

Bruno didn't answer, instead turning to leave the kitchen. Pepa reached for him, her hand clutching his arm and holding him back. For a moment at least.

"I love you so much, Bruno. That will never change," she said, her voice softening. "I could never be so mad at you, so angry that I wouldn't want you in my life. You're part of me, like Julieta is, like we are to you. Please remember that. Please think of us and let us help you. Don't turn us away."

Bruno nodded but said nothing.

He gently pulled his arm away and walked out of the kitchen.

CHAPTER
SIXTEEN

The line seemed to extend past the Encanto, past the mountains that cordoned off the magical town from the rest of Colombia. People had come from every part of the village. The baker, one of the teachers, parents and their children, everyone—all waiting for a chance to talk to Bruno. To get a taste of what their future might hold.

Bruno swallowed hard. Was this truly a good idea?

Then the vision reappeared in his mind. Of a possible future where Bruno was alone. Hiding. Lurking in the dark corners of Casita. A pariah to his family, friends, and life. Surely this was to become a reality if he stayed on the path he was on? He had to do what he could to prevent that vision from becoming reality—even if it meant acting in a way that didn't feel comfortable. Or using his gift in ways he wasn't used to.

The first person to approach Bruno was Irina Lujo, a young woman about Bruno's age. Her parents lived on the other side of town. Simple folk, her father was a carpenter and her mother a midwife. Good people who worked hard and gave what they could for the betterment of Encanto. Bruno liked them, but he had to admit he rarely thought of them. A pang of guilt hit him before Irina spoke.

"Bruno, thank you for seeing me."

He nodded slowly, unsure if this was truly the best strategy. But he'd already started, and he couldn't stop now.

"It's . . . well, it's about my family—my parents," Irina said haltingly. "They have this future in mind for me. This person. They want me to marry José, a family friend. He is a good man. Works hard, like my father. He is kind and loves me, but . . ."

"You don't know if you feel the same way," Bruno said.

Irina frowned.

"No, I know I don't feel the same way," she said firmly. "I love him as a friend. But I am not . . .

interested in him. In marriage. I feel like I'm still discovering who I am. I feel too young. Too inexperienced. Tell me, Bruno—am I going to end up with José? Do I need to brace for that? Is there something I can do?"

Bruno was still figuring out how this could work. His instinct, his natural inclination, was to look into his mind—to produce a vision that would just answer Irina's question. But he was different now, and he wanted to give hope, not deliver bad news. He closed his eyes. He let his mind drift. The vision appeared for him. He hadn't really asked for it, but it felt almost like muscle memory. He saw Irina, in a small, cramped house. Surrounded by children. Her husband leaving early in the morning to go to work as she watched him, a tiny baby resting on her as two smaller children ran around in the background. She looked tired, exhausted—like a person who had poured herself into a life she was not excited about. The dark bags under her eyes told Bruno that Irina didn't sleep much. She waved goodbye to José.

Bruno opened his eyes and looked at Irina. He tried to smile.

"What?" she asked. "What do you see?"

Bruno took a deep breath. He felt a sharp sense of dread. Every time he did this, it seemed to grow stronger. In the past it had come easily—he would just share what he saw and let the chips fall where they might. But if he told Irina the truth here, she would be upset. Not only at the world, but at Bruno. She would push him further away. Her anger would fuel his eventual transformation into that dark, lurking Bruno he never wanted to be. He wanted to help her, too. If he told her something else—something she wanted to hear—what would the harm be in that?

Bruno met her eyes.

"You won't marry José," he said softly. "You need to stand firm, but you will not be forced to marry him. Your future is bright. Light and easy. That is all I see now."

Her body slammed into his as she pulled him into a long, tight hug.

"Oh, Bruno, thank you, thank you," she said, her voice muffled by his shirt. He knew she was crying, too. "I needed to hear that. I felt so trapped. I felt like my future was locked in and I would be sentenced to this life no matter what. Thank you."

She pulled back and looked up at him. She gave him a quick peck on the cheek and turned around, looking back to wave at him as the next person stepped up to talk to Bruno.

Bruno waved back and smiled. Or thought he did. He felt his mouth turning upward, the muscles moving in accordance with what a smile looked like. But this was different. This was something else.

He was pretending.

෧\෧෧\෧෧\෧

It had been a long day, and Bruno thought he was done. But one more person remained. He recognized Francisco Padilla immediately.

The older man pulled back his hood slowly as he stepped up to the entrance of Casita. His expression was stoic and stern.

"Bruno," he said with a nod.

"Hello, my friend," Bruno said with a wan smile. He was tired. He'd spoken to so many people today, lifted so many spirits—but the work itself was exhausting. He couldn't just give people platitudes and empty promises. He had to spend time really digging and thinking about what they wanted to hear. How many puppies would Maria Alcanara's dog have? Was Jaime the carpenter going to get a decent apprentice this season? Did Chef Solorzano have all the ingredients he'd need for the annual town feast? Who was the person Doña Morales kept seeing wandering around the edges of Encanto? Would the crops be enough to allow for the Mendoza farm to sustain itself? Bruno had worked hard— making sure the visions he claimed he was seeing were based in fact and that the information they gave his visitors not only sounded true—but also sounded *good*. He wanted to give people hope. Real hope. So far, it felt like he'd been succeeding. Until Francisco Padilla arrived.

"You are the talk of Encanto, Bruno," Padilla said, taking a seat across from Bruno.

They were in the foyer of Casita, in two chairs facing each other a few feet from the main entrance. The area had basically become Bruno's ad hoc sitting room—where he welcomed visitors and shared his visions.

"That's good," Bruno said with that fake smile. He tilted his head for effect. This was the new him. Relaxed. Happy. Excited. He saw Padilla stiffen in response.

"Perhaps," the older man said. "But I have to ask—why are you suddenly sharing your gift? Before, it seemed like you'd see visions and share as they happened, if they happened. Now . . . you're holding court."

Bruno waited. He could tell Padilla had more to say.

He was right.

"The last time I saw you, Bruno, you were struggling—something was eating at you, I could tell. I hoped I had given you useful advice, but it seems—"

"Seems what?" Bruno said. His face heated. He was ashamed. But why? He was doing what he thought was right, wasn't he? "I'm just trying to help people."

Padilla nodded, more to himself than Bruno.

"I know, mijo, but this is not the way," Padilla said with a defeated shrug. "I'm hearing from everyone that you've told them their wildest hopes and dreams are coming true. What happens, Bruno, when those things don't appear?"

"What's the harm?" Bruno asked. "My whole life, I've been a gray cloud—the bearer of bad news. I've been the person who lets you know your cat is dying or that the clouds are about to burst on your wedding. Why can't I share something good for a change?"

Padilla let out a short sigh.

"It's not that simple."

"Why not?" Bruno said, standing up and stepping toward the older man. "I'm tired of being a weirdo. The guy people avoid. I want to be loved. Embraced and cheered on. I'm not looking at the future and changing my mind. I'm just giving people what they want. It might even be right!"

Padilla frowned.

"It is most definitely not right, Bruno," Padilla said, looking Bruno over. "I know, deep down, underneath the new clothes, your new hairstyle, your new speech patterns—you understand that, too."

Bruno's throat tightened.

"This is what you told me to do," Bruno said, his words hurried—as if trying to escape before the doors closed on them. "You said as much."

"I said no such thing," Padilla responded, standing up to face Bruno, his expression stricken with surprise. "How did you come to that conclusion?"

Bruno didn't have time to answer. He turned to see his mami stepping down Casita's main stairs toward them. She looked like she'd seen un fantasma.

"Francisco Padilla, te dije mil veces—do not ever enter this house," Alma said, her voice rising with each word, each step granting her more volume as she got closer. Bruno felt a jolt of fear. He had never seen his mother like this—irrationally angry. "Lárgate, Francisco—no lo voy a repetir."

Padilla seemed to fold into himself, suddenly looking shy and sheepish. He didn't respond to Alma's sharp words, instead pulling his hood over his head and turning to Bruno.

"You are walking down a dangerous path, niño," the older man said, his eyes glassy and . . . scared? "The magic of Encanto is a precious thing. It is not something you can tinker with and tweak at your convenience. By doing what you're doing, you're putting everything your mother built at risk."

He turned and walked toward the door. Annoyance built up in him. Who was this man to come to his house and lecture Bruno about his choices?

"How dare you!" Bruno said. He could sense his mother next to him, looking up at him. "Come here and tell me what I should do? I'm doing what I was taught—I'm using my gift to help people. To do good."

Padilla spun around, one foot out the door.

"Well, you know what they say about the best intentions, Bruno," he said gravely. "I wish you well, always, mi amigo."

The door slammed behind Padilla. Bruno's body sagged, and he felt his mother's hand on his arm.

"Es una fuerza mala, ese hombre," she said, patting Bruno's arm. "I don't know why you speak to him."

"I won't, Mami. Not anymore," Bruno said. "He's no longer my friend."

CHAPTER
SEVENTEEN

This is what I wanted. What I needed to happen.

The visions had to be questionable. Doubted.

If Bruno truly saw the future, my plan would die a quick death.

But now, now the future is uncertain. My pathways clouded. My methods obfuscated by his own power. All for a few smiles and hugs from strangers.

The further Bruno got from himself, the greater the distance between him and his own powers, the higher my chances of success. The more likely that Encanto would fall.

And a dark cloud would envelop La Casa Madrigal and all its residents.

CHAPTER

EIGHTEEN

The soft rain seemed apt, Bruno thought, as he dodged puddles and made his way toward silence. Toward space. Toward some kind of quiet that could allow him a few moments to breathe.

Casita was no longer the place for that. Bruno was overstimulated and distracted, even within the confines of his room—which had always been his safe, comfortable place. The line of people, ever present outside Casita, made it impossible to go in unnoticed. And inside, the entire house was turned upside down, with his sisters preparing feverishly for Mami's upcoming birthday celebration—an event that would involve everyone in Encanto. Bruno needed to be somewhere else. He needed to think.

He had tried to ignore the thoughts buzzing

around his mind about Pepa and her husband. Had chalked it up to his own anxiety and irrational thoughts, but perhaps they were more than fleeting ideas. He'd run into Pepa just as he'd stepped out of Casita. Normally he'd just walk by with a wave, but something drove him to pause—and it hadn't just been the stern look on her face.

"Hi, Pepa," Bruno had said, trying to be friendly. He had to remind himself that they'd talked recently, that she'd told him plainly she was fine, that she'd gotten over any anger from Bruno's vision on her wedding day. But that didn't seem true right then.

"Don't 'hi, Pepa' me, Bruno," she said, brow furrowing. "You have a lot of nerve stepping out of the house right now."

Bruno's skin went cold. His sister seemed so upset, so focused on him. His anxiety spiked, showing him different versions of what was about to happen. None of them good. He had to leave. Now.

"Bruno, Julieta and I have been doing all the planning for Mami's party—where are you going?" Pepa said, her voice sharp. "We could really use your help."

But Bruno wasn't listening. Her tone and expression had tapped a nerve and sent him down another path, one that wasn't built on the rational. He didn't recall if he'd responded.

He remembered sidestepping Pepa and speeding away from Casita, her voice rising behind him. But he hadn't listened. He couldn't. Who knew what he'd realize if he did?

So much had happened in such a short time, Bruno thought, it was getting harder and harder to keep up. He really wanted to do the right thing—he had to. He needed to avoid the future he had seen for himself, and that meant preventing himself from becoming the Bruno he'd seen—isolated, hidden, lonely. He understood, in theory, what Padilla was saying—but what if his mami was right? What if Francisco Padilla had his own motives? It was too much.

Bruno reached the clearing—a small patch of land a few yards away from the edge of Encanto. Nondescript and forgettable by most standards, but special to him, even in the light drizzle. The lush green grass seemed endless except for the small hill that jutted out a few feet in front of Bruno. It felt like a sacred, secret spot. A place Bruno would visit at times like these—when he was looking for some time to just be. To think. Similar to the crevices in his own house, he thought.

No, not them.

He couldn't go back there, he reasoned. No matter the comfort that isolation brought. No matter the peace he seemed to find. He was someone else now. He didn't need to hide. He wanted to be with people, surrounded by them—he wanted to bring them joy and be a positive force in Encanto. Not a dark omen.

But Padilla's words nagged at him. What was the older man getting at? Didn't he understand why Bruno needed to do this? Bruno sat down at the base of the hill and let his head hang down.

If he was becoming this new person, Bruno wondered, why did he feel so alone?

The rush of helping should've lasted longer. The joy that came from giving his neighbors and friends hope and energy should have done the same for him. Instead, he felt like an empty vessel. But perhaps it was too soon to judge what was happening. Yes, that was it. Bruno had to keep at it. He had to continue to change himself to save Encanto. To save his family. To become the person Alma, Pepa, and Julieta wanted him to be—to be the person his community needed. Otherwise, he'd become that frightening visage, and Bruno could not stomach that.

But the vision of himself wasn't the only sign

that was troubling Bruno this rainy afternoon. The other vision he'd seen before—felt more than seen, really—popped back into his mind. That deep, painful sense of regret and betrayal. The idea that someone close to him would not only abandon Bruno but hurt him and Encanto, as well. Bruno sat with his feelings a bit longer, trying to dig into the vision, but nothing came. Bruno knew his gift was mysterious and not prone to being managed or instigated, but still, he'd hoped for some clarity. Perhaps he was just tired.

Who would betray him? Who would abandon Bruno to benefit themselves?

Alma appeared in his mind. Then Julieta. Then Pepa. He loved them. But of all the people he knew, aside from Padilla, their reactions to his change had been the sharpest. Hadn't they *wanted* him to be more like them? Friendlier? Jovial? Outspoken? Social? But when Bruno had started to do those things—when he started to use his gift to help people and when he changed his appearance and how he carried himself—the first people raising questions were his mother and sisters.

Bruno rubbed his eyes. He was tired. Physically and emotionally. This was not a good time to drill down and figure out who was behind the betrayal he'd felt. He just needed time alone, to breathe—to not be talking. To not be listening. The act—or, rather, the evolution—that being Bruno had become was exhausting. He could admit that to himself here, alone beside this hill, without anyone to perform for. Would it always be this way? Had he sentenced himself to a life of pretending and acting to save his family and home? If that was the case, so be it.

It finally came to him with a jolt as he let out a long, exhausted sigh. The vision again. Of a dark, looming cloud hanging over the Encanto. Of a lingering, deep sense of betrayal. A feeling that someone he loved and trusted was going to change and leave Bruno alone. His eyes widened as the vision deepened, the view pulling him down from the gray-tinged skies to the ground, where the people of the village seemed frantic, running around in a panic. He felt the calm, peaceful tone of his home disrupted—perhaps forever—by some unseen force. Someone Bruno knew well.

But who? he thought, his mind screaming the question, the words bouncing around his head as the vision faded.

His thoughts jumped to his family again. They

seemed like the obvious choice. Could it be one of them? Could Bruno, in his haste to do the right thing, have wronged them somehow? The idea seemed alien to him—but so much had left him unmoored and distracted. Could he be wrong about this, too?

He took a minute to catch his ragged breath, his entire mind and body still reeling from the vision. He studied his hands. They were shaking. As he looked up, he noticed a figure approaching through the clearing.

It was Roberto, waving playfully, a smile on his face, seeming completely unbothered by the weather. Unlike Bruno, Roberto was prepared—umbrella in hand. The rain had gotten stronger, Bruno realized. His friend reached the clearing and sat down next to him without a word.

"I just needed some time to myself," Bruno said, trying to predict what Roberto would ask.

"No te preocupes," Roberto said with a smile. "You don't need to predict everything I'm going to do."

They laughed. It was an easy, heartfelt laugh. Bruno needed this, he realized, to be around someone he liked and trusted without any pretense.

"The town is all about Bruno Madrigal," Roberto said, looking out at the clearing. "You're making people happy."

"I hope so," Bruno said, kicking a small rock absent-mindedly. "I want people to feel good. I want the town's energy to stay positive."

"Your sister is worried about you. Julieta—"

"She has nothing to worry about," Bruno said curtly. "I know how to take care of myself. She's only older by a few seconds."

Roberto smiled as he turned to look at Bruno.

"She loves you," he said. "That's all."

Bruno looked down at his feet.

"I know, but if she really does, she needs to leave me alone. Let me work on this my way."

"Work on what, though? I mean, I think it's good that you're, I dunno, coming out and being yourself more—but is it because you want to?" Roberto said. "Or because you feel like you have to?"

Bruno didn't have an answer for that.

Roberto grabbed Bruno by the shoulder playfully, surprising him.

"Bruno, we need to loosen up, okay?"

"What do you mean?" Bruno asked, looking down at Roberto's hand on his shoulder.

"You're so serious, amigo," Roberto said, smiling, eyes wide. "I know what that's like. I know what it is to be alone. To feel like you don't have a place. But we do have a place. A place that we create. Does that make sense?"

Bruno nodded hesitatingly.

"I think so?"

"You know so," Roberto said. "We can't just sit around feeling sad about the world, or bummed because not everyone approves of who we are. What kind of life is that?"

Roberto released him and stood up, his eyes still on Bruno.

"I felt alone for a long time. I didn't feel like I had a place here in Encanto," Roberto said, motioning toward the town. "But then I realized I had to make my own space, build my own relationships—and be myself. But be a version of myself that was fun, lighthearted, and easy."

"You . . . pretended?" Bruno asked as he stood up, too.

Roberto let out a low laugh.

"No, not at all," he said. "I just decided to be myself, and to let things happen. People would want to be happy around me because I was already happy.

If you're sad, you attract the same. I think there's something to be learned there, no? Don't you feel like you're outside of everything else?"

Bruno thought for a moment. He couldn't deny Roberto's words.

"Sometimes."

"Well, there you go," Roberto said with a playful shrug. "Tell me more."

Bruno hesitated, the fear looming before him. But then he closed his eyes for a moment and spoke.

"I just feel . . . I just feel like sometimes I'm too different," Bruno said, his voice catching. "Like no one cares about me because I'm not like them. I'm just . . . outside of the world. A different kind of person."

"You are different," Roberto said, his voice low. "But that's what makes you special."

Bruno pulled away. The two friends smiled at each other, as if a deep lesson had been shared. The silence seemed to bolster their feelings of friendship and support. Bruno felt less alone. And that meant the world to him.

"Thank you. That means a lot. But . . . can we talk about something else?" Bruno asked, a dry smile on his face. "Like, when are you going to propose to my sister?"

Bruno gently elbowed his friend, who responded with a low chuckle.

"You tell me, Bruno," he said. "She knows I care about her."

"Mami is eager for Julieta to get married, to make the family bigger and stronger," Bruno said. "But I don't know if Julieta wants that to happen right now, just because Pepa is married. It's a lot of pressure. Not just from Mami, but from the town. Everyone in Encanto looks to Mami for leadership. We don't run the town, but we are central to it. Mami believes the stronger the family is, the longer the magic—and the gifts—will last. If we don't keep strengthening the family, the candle could flicker."

"What do you believe?"

Bruno shrugged.

"I think we should all do what we want," he said, as much to himself as his friend. "I think Julieta likes you, but I don't think she wants to get married tomorrow. Pepa is different. She wants to keep Mami happy and she wants a family now."

"And what do you want?"

Bruno turned to his friend, looking into his dark eyes.

"I want to be safe. I want to be appreciated," he said. The words stung as he spoke them, as if pulled directly from his heart. "I want people to love me for who I am—not what they want me to be."

Roberto placed a hand on Bruno's shoulder.

"You are loved, Bruno," Roberto said. "By your family, the town, me. We all admire you. I respect you for what you're doing. Trying to help people feel confident and happy. You're bringing joy to a place that has been a home to you. It's admirable."

"Then why are so many people criticizing me?"

"You mean Padilla?" Roberto said, his tone suddenly darkening. "I've heard the gossip about him, and what he said to you. But listen . . . he's a crackpot, Bruno. I don't even know why you talk to him. He has no magic, no gift—but walks around the town like he knows something we don't. He's dangerous. Even your mother says so."

Bruno nodded. He knew how Roberto felt about Padilla but had never heard him spell it out so clearly. But that wasn't what he'd been asking.

"I mean my family," Bruno said. "If they love me so much, why are they so opposed to me doing this? It's for their own good."

Roberto nodded.

"Just give them time," Roberto said. "Okay? Families are often set in their ways. They need to get used to the new you."

Bruno stood up. The movement was so quick and sudden that Roberto stepped back, as if dodging a blow.

"I don't have time," Bruno said. "Something bad is coming—and I can't tell what it's going to be. I need to be ready. And I need to make sure my family is safe. My town is safe. This is the best way to guarantee that."

Roberto moved toward him, but Bruno sidestepped his friend. The rain had stopped.

"I need some time to think," Bruno said. "I need to be alone."

Roberto nodded.

"That's fine," he said. "Do whatever you need."

Bruno smiled at his friend. He appreciated him. The blind support and kindness. It felt so new and different. So unlike the couched comments and judgment that seemed so commonplace with his family. Why was that? he wondered.

Roberto started to walk back toward the town.

"Hang in there, Bruno," he said with a gentle wave. "We love you. You'll be okay. Keep doing what you're doing."

Bruno waved back and watched Roberto wander away. He felt validated. Finally, someone appreciated him—someone was rooting for him and *understood* why he was doing what he was doing. It was refreshing.

Bruno sat back down. He closed his eyes. He had two things to figure out: who was going to betray him and Encanto, and if his own future had changed thanks to his actions over the past few days. He'd try to figure out the first one now.

He took a deep breath. He let his mind's eye come into focus, as the gift had worked so many times before. He waited. Waited for the vision to form and for the clues to cement into place.

But nothing happened.

He felt the familiar flicker—a feeling so personal and impossible to explain that Bruno had just accepted it for what it was, something that only he could do. The gift he'd been given. But after that—there was nothing.

The vision in front of him remained foggy, like gray smoke swirling around—but that was all. The sense of betrayal lingered, but it was even less focused than before. He couldn't make anything out. But he knew where he was—in Casita, with that sense of abandonment sharper than ever before. But why couldn't he *see* anything now?

Bruno felt his mind staring into the vision, which was like white noise—static and smoke.

Until a form appeared. A dark shape. A face.

Bruno's vision crept closer to the shape. Saw it looming, but Bruno couldn't make out who it was. Before he could try to focus, before he could try to look more closely, the face seemed to notice him.

And it screamed in anger.

Excerpt from Julieta Madrigal's Diary

I've tried to avoid writing this, but it's been going on long enough that I have to admit it.

I think Bruno is in trouble.

Last night, I saw Agustín and handed him one of my empanadas. I knew he'd fallen off his horse—as he does at least once a week—that morning. I went by his house to help him feel better. It's our bond. I like helping him. He's sweet and kind, and also sweet on me. I want him to feel better. He ate it, as he normally does, and it worked. He suddenly felt better. But instead of feeling joyous and free about it, I felt a great sadness. Because while I could help Agustín with food, why couldn't I help Bruno? I can see my hermanito struggling—trying to be everything to everyone—and that path only promises pain to him. But can a plate of food fix his pain if it comes from within? Unfortunately, no.

I wanted to talk to Mami about it, because it's the kind of thing she should know. But she's been so

busy. Bustling around Casita, trying to pretend she doesn't see our plans for her birthday. Why add to the drama? I thought. Pepa is so immersed in the party planning with Félix away helping his parents on their farm that it's hard to talk to her, either.

And what about Bruno? Do I talk to him? Reach out my hand to help? Where do I even begin? My poor hermanito seems endlessly stressed, trying to help everyone in town—but is he really helping? Is he really seeing those things he's sharing? I don't know. And if he knows he's lying . . . what does that mean about him? About us and our town?

It's a lot, dear diary.

But I will have to talk to them. Soon. Because the longer we're all divided—the longer we ignore that something bad is brewing—the more it means all of Encanto is in danger. And we can't risk that.

CHAPTER
NINETEEN

Bruno's eyes flickered open and he realized where he was. In the clearing. Lying on his back in the rain-soaked grass.

His head ached. His entire body seemed to throb. What had happened?

Had he fallen asleep? Had he been knocked out?

The static and smoke seemed to converge into more concrete images in his mind. He remembered bits and pieces from the half-baked vision he'd sought out, trying to find out who was going to betray him and Encanto.

The darkening skies. The looming, massive cloud casting a long shadow over Casita, Encanto. The faces of his friends, neighbors, classmates—everyone. But where was his family? He'd seen them—or thought he did. First as silhouettes, forms approaching him, muttering words he couldn't make out. Then dissipating into dust as Bruno tried to reach out to them. Was that Pepa? Julieta? Mami? The shapes kept morphing, changing—familiar ones, strange ones. Bruno couldn't keep up—his mind spinning frantically. Who were the people standing outside of Casita, pulsing with dangerous energy—the cause of what was happening? Why did he feel so helpless?

One figure in particular approached. Bruno had strained his eyes trying to make out who it was—but before the picture became clear, everything went black.

Then the scream.

Bruno shook his head, trying to shake the vision back—to get one more chance to see who he needed to stop. But it didn't return. Only an empty void remained.

What was going on? Bruno wondered. Not only with his world, but with his gift?

He got up slowly, shakily, and wandered back to Encanto. He knew who he had to talk to, even if it was the last person he wanted to see.

CHAPTER
TWENTY

"**M**ami?"

Alma Madrigal turned at the sound of Bruno's voice. He was standing outside of her study. He'd realized as he took the stairs up to see his mami that he was soaking wet, his clothes dirty and disheveled. He could only imagine what she was thinking as she saw him. He didn't have to imagine for long, as her concern spread across her face.

"Come in, Bruno," she said softly.

He did, taking a seat on the small couch behind her desk. She moved her chair to face him. The room was sparsely decorated—but it felt very much like his mami. Tidy, organized, but also entrenched in the mysterious and unknown. Behind her was a large painting of Encanto that Mami had become very fond of, done by a local artist. It put front and center Alma Madrigal's main concern: her people, her town, and the preservation of a certain vision of it. It was, in some ways, what Bruno had come to talk to her about.

"It's late, mijo. Debes dormir," she said. Small talk. She knew he was here to talk about something serious. Her children rarely entered this particular sanctum, preferring to laugh and chat in more common areas, like the kitchen and dining room, over food or drinks. This was where work got done, though.

"I'm not tired, Mami," he said. Even Bruno could hear how deflated he sounded. He didn't know where else to turn. He needed help, and she was the first person who'd come to mind. "I need to talk to you."

Alma nodded, waiting for Bruno to continue.

"It's my gift, Mami—it's . . . how do I say this . . . ?"

"Speak truly, Bruno," Alma said.

Bruno had so much he wanted to say. But the words seemed to stall. He wanted to tell his mami that his gift felt less reliable, that the more times he envisioned what he thought people wanted, the harder it became to actually see what the future held. His gift was there—he knew it—but clouded behind something. But how could he say this to his mami?

"Are you worried about your gift?" Alma said. "Whether it will be with you always?"

Bruno sat up straight.

"How . . . how do you know this?"

"I can sense it, mi niño," Alma said, a humorless smile on her face. "The same way I can sense that something is troubling you, Bruno. There is no way to know that your gift will be here forever, but it is your responsibility to do whatever you can to hold on to it. You must allow it to thrive. You must tend to it. Are you doing that?"

"I . . . I think so? I'm not sure," Bruno said. "I'm trying to use it to do good. I'm trying to be more like the person you want me to be."

Alma's eyes glazed over, the sheen of tears evident even from across the room.

"Bruno, I just want you to be happy," she said, leaning forward. "Can you tell me what's happening? How can I help you?"

"Someone is going to betray Encanto," he said

flatly, watching his mami carefully. "Someone is trying to hurt us, and I can't see who it is. My powers won't let me see it."

Alma leaned back in her seat, hands folded in her lap.

"But you saw more before," she said. It wasn't a question. "And now you see it less clearly?"

"Yes, it's harder to figure out—like a fog has descended on my visions," Bruno said, clutching his head like a child trying to avoid a lecture. "I feel like I'm losing myself."

"Did you ever think, though, that perhaps the vision is getting harder to see—because it's not going to come true?"

Bruno had thought of this, of course, but the scream—the frightening shadowy face he'd witnessed—seemed to challenge that idea.

Before he could respond, Alma continued.

"Your gifts are not like water from a bucket—the same wherever you pour it," she said. "It's magic, Bruno. Something we will never understand. But I do know that the gifts work when you are feeling most connected to yourself. But you seem worried—distant, even as you try to be someone else."

"I'm just being myself," Bruno said tersely. This was not going the way he'd hoped. "I want my gift to help—not upset people."

"Who is upset?"

"You," Bruno snapped. "You and Pepa, and everyone."

"Pepa? Your sister was upset because she told me you weren't helping set up for this party they're planning—but that's normal, Bruno," Alma said with a wave of her hand. "She said you just ran off before she could say anything. Is that really what's bothering you?"

"No, it's just an example," Bruno said. "It's bigger than that, okay? Any time I saw something, I'd share it—trying to be helpful. But as time passed, no one wanted to hear from me. I became a pariah. Even though I was just trying to help people. Trying to be present for them."

Alma didn't flinch at Bruno's raised voice.

"And now?"

"Now . . . I feel like I'm helping people," Bruno lied. He did feel helpful, but he didn't feel good—which he realized was his mother's point. But he was not ready to give in on that front. "They come to me with their problems and I can give them a brief break."

Alma stood up and straightened her worn gray dress.

"I want you to be happy, Bruno," she said, looking at the floor. "I want you to feel loved and to love. Perhaps I have not made that as clear to you as I should have. But your gift is a precious and delicate thing. You should be careful with how you use it. Listening to grifters like Padilla—that will not help anyone."

"I'm not talking to him anymore," Bruno said flatly.

Alma nodded as she began pacing around the small room.

"If someone betrays us, betrays Encanto, we have to be ready—to protect ourselves and the magic of Casita at all costs," she said sternly. "There is nothing more important."

"But what if it's not an external threat, Mami?"

Alma's brow furrowed.

"What do you mean?"

"What if our own family is the problem?" Bruno said, hands outstretched. "What if, through our own actions, we're betraying what this town stands for?"

Alma's stricken expression would be burned into Bruno's memory for the rest of his life.

⊙⊙⊙⊙⊙

"Bruno! Bruno!"

He heard Señora Anta's voice from across the town square, and his throat tightened. She sounded frantic, he thought.

The rain had been replaced by a blazing sun, the kind that seemed to envelop Encanto in moments—drying the puddles and lighting up the small town like a holiday ornament. But Bruno wasn't worried about that now.

"Hola, Señora Anta," Bruno said as the older woman approached him, her eyes wild, her movements jagged. "¿Cómo estás?"

"Bueno, Bruno. I am . . . estoy muy bien," she said, choking back a sob. Bruno was at a loss. "Es que . . . Julio. He's fine! He is okay! He's walking and doing better than before. It's a miracle."

Bruno opened his mouth to answer, but she kept going.

"I was scared to talk to you, because so many—well, some people have said you only see the bad," she said. "But when you told me Julio would be fine—I wanted to believe it so much. I wanted him to be okay. I wanted it to be true. And now it is, you see? You were right, Bruno. You saved his life. You gave me hope when I needed it."

She was leaning into him now, her hands clutching his, her body almost collapsing in front of him. He didn't know what to do. He was speechless and confused. *Had* he been right? Had he somehow tapped into a different way to use his powers? Or had he been lucky?

"Well, I am so . . . uh . . . I am so glad to hear that," he said, still trying to remain cool, to seem like the new, personable Bruno. But he was having trouble. His head felt light. His entire body felt like it was spinning. "I'm so happy for you, Señora."

She pulled him in for a long hug, her tear-stained face wet on his cheek. She was saying something else, but Bruno couldn't hear anymore. He grew distant, his eyes looking out toward the other side of town. Toward a figure looming, backlit by the powerful sun. He knew who it was. He didn't need to be any closer to recognize Francisco Padilla, his long green cloak flapping in the slight breeze.

Bruno looked down for a second to pat Señora Anta's arm, but when he looked up again—Padilla was gone. Had Bruno imagined the older man being there?

He shook the thought from his mind and allowed himself to enjoy the moment.

To enjoy not only being right, but being appreciated.

CHAPTER
TWENTY-ONE

"I'm just worried I failed that test."

Antonia's words hung between her and Bruno as they both sat under the makeshift tent. It'd been a week since Bruno's encounter with Señora Anta, and this was to be a banner day—his first in the town square as part of the weekly farmers market. He'd set it all up sheepishly, with some help from Roberto. A table, the tent, a small inconspicuous sign that read YOUR FUTURE IS HERE, and two chairs. He didn't want money or favors. He just wanted to help people.

His recent conversation with Señora Anta had cemented it for Bruno. Something had changed in him, and even if he wasn't sure what it was—he knew it was real. He could somehow tap into the future and make it into something else, he realized.

Something good. The hope he was creating in Encanto was palpable. People were smiling at each other. Songs were being sung in the town square. The odd stares were gone, replaced by warm smiles and eager eyes.

Bruno was different, too. The act he'd been putting on felt more natural now. Still like wearing a different skin, but repetition bred some level of comfort. Bruno knew how to play the part. Eventually, he mused, the role would become who he was. The transformation would be complete, and the old shy, awkward, strange Bruno would be a distant memory few would even want to think back on.

It was only a matter of time.

"You passed, don't worry," Bruno said, patting the younger teenager's clasped hands gently. Immediately, her expression changed—from a worried frown to a beaming smile. She got up, arms raised. Unsure what to do with herself, she gave Bruno a quick, awkward hug.

"Oh, Bruno, thank you, thank you! This is a miracle," she said excitedly as she ran from the tent. "The future is bright here."

Bruno motioned for the next person to sit with

him. He looked up to see his sister Pepa. She did not look happy.

"Mami is worried," she said, her words an annoyed drone. "What is this, Bruno? This tent? This whole thing?"

She waved her arms around as if Bruno hadn't seen the structure—hadn't set up the tent himself. She looked more agitated than usual.

"Pepa, you seem—"

"I don't seem, hermanito, I *am* worried. About you. About what you're doing and how it's affecting Mami, about everything," she said, leaning forward, looking conspiratorial. "Something is off. I can feel it."

She tapped her chest. She didn't mean a vague feeling with no base; she meant inside—her gift. Bruno heard the rumble of thunder in the distance.

"What we have, Bruno—what the magic of Encanto gifted us—is special," she said, tilting her head in his direction. "We don't know how long it lasts, or if it may disappear tomorrow, you know? We could wake up one morning and the magic could be fading. We must all be true to this special thing."

Bruno shook his head.

"Pepa, do you even know me?"

She scoffed.

"Know you? We were in the womb together, li'l bro—I love you like I love Julieta and myself," she said, pointing a finger at Bruno. "We're cut from the same cloth, Bruno. I'm here because I want to help you."

Bruno leaned back in his chair. He could still feel the discomfort of the new shirt he'd purchased at Señor Rodriguez's store, the tightness in the legs of the new pair of slacks he was wearing. Everything felt uncomfortable. Out of sorts. His quest to become a new Bruno had stalled, but he hadn't given up. He couldn't. Too many people were relying on him.

He took in a short breath.

"This is how you can help me," Bruno said, motioning toward the line of people waiting outside the tent, looking at them with eager, hungry eyes. "You can go home to your husband, you can keep the weather nice and sunny, and you can talk to Mami. You can tell her not to worry. That the Bruno she worried about? That shy, nervous, and awkward kid? He's gone. I'm different now. I'm confident. I'm happy. I'm loving my life and using my gift to help the people around me. And I am fine."

Pepa's mouth flattened into a thin line.

"I need you to trust me on this, Pepa," he said, patting her hand gingerly. "It's doing some real good. People are happy. The energy of Encanto is back. It feels like I'm a kid again. The joy . . . I can feel it."

Another crack of thunder. Bruno could hear light droplets of rain landing on the tent. He looked at his sister. Her expression had only gotten more dour. Pepa stood up in one swift movement and stepped toward the edge of the tent.

"Remember Javi Alfaro, Bruno?" she asked. "You went to school with his brother Erik."

"Yes, I saw him not long ago—he was worried about overfeeding his goldfish," Bruno said with a slight chuckle. The laugh fizzled when he saw Pepa's expression. "Why?"

"That fish died," Pepa said, one eyebrow raised. "Javi came home after talking to you to find it floating in its tank. After you promised him the fish would live for quite some time. That it was just fine. That he shouldn't worry—you'd seen it in your vision."

Bruno shrugged, tried to play it off—but a shiver was overcoming him.

"Bueno, Pepa, what can I say? I don't ever tell people

that my visions are one hundred percent accurate," he said, stammering slightly. "Javi knew that—"

Pepa stepped forward and leaned over Bruno, bringing their faces closer. Her eyes were locked on his, her hands on his shoulders.

"No one reads the fine print," she said. "No one listens to disclaimers. They want hope. They want to be told everything will be fine. They want to *believe*. It's what Encanto is built on. This idea that magic can bring us together and give us a chance at a better, happier life. But what you're doing? Whatever it is? You're messing with the heart of this town—and it's not going to end well, Bruno. You need to stop. Before you hurt someone even worse with these fake visions and promises."

She'd gone too far. Bruno stood up, shrugging away Pepa's touch. Anger coursed through him—along with shame and embarrassment. Was he mad at her, he wondered, or himself?

"Pepa, you need to leave," he said.

But his sister was already gone.

CHAPTER
TWENTY-TWO

My plan is working. The results are greater than even I anticipated. Even I, who have been here since the dawning of Encanto. Never in my wildest dreams did I think this was even possible. I have weakened him so much, he's losing touch with the very gift that defined him.

I watch his sister storm out of the tent. Watch as the gray storm cloud follows her, with little flickers of lightning and thunder like a weak child's toy. I sense the joy—the sudden happiness—that Bruno created slowly morphing. Turning into something else. Something toxic and bad. People wanted to believe him, but now they are starting to doubt him. They will soon hate him. Nothing built on lies can do good for very long, no matter the original intent. Soon they will be at their most vulnerable—doubting not only themselves but each other.

And then I will strike. I will pull back my cloak and reveal myself—and then my vengeance will be complete.

CHAPTER
TWENTY-THREE

Was this what happiness was? It had been so long since he had truly felt happy that he had forgotten what it was like.

Bruno wondered this as he tried to move, tried to *dance*, even. The band's music was loud and adventurous, and it seemed like the entire town was out in front of Casita, dancing and singing together to celebrate a day that had become close to a holiday for all Encanto's residents: Alma Madrigal's birthday.

Julieta, Pepa, and—to a much lesser degree—Bruno had pulled out all the stops, doing their best to ensure that their mother felt not only admired but loved and appreciated. People from every corner of Encanto came with both presents and stories— memories of Alma, of her brave journey and the magic she'd brought forth to start the town and the house at its center. The tales were heartfelt and true, and Bruno was impressed to see a side of his mother he'd only imagined—a young woman left widowed by violence, who instead of folding into herself pressed on and became a legend. The stories ranged from the comical to the anecdotal to the inspirational—and Bruno could see his mami's face glowing from her seat in front of Casita as she listened intently to the many people she'd had a positive effect on. Bruno thought he'd seen a single tear streak down her cheek, but he couldn't be sure. Olga Deju shared how Alma had helped her move into her small house with no complaint, Karina Menendez offered up an inspiring tale of Alma vouching for her to a shopkeeper when she desperately needed a job, and there were no dry eyes visible when Julieta and Pepa took turns sharing their admiration for Mami. Bruno had been ready to go next—the loose script scribbled on a small piece of paper coated with sweat and hastily tucked into his back pocket—when he approached his mother's seat. She was in a heated conversation with another woman, someone Bruno thought looked familiar but couldn't place. She was white-haired and frail-looking, but moved with a spry energy that Bruno found disconcerting. He had wanted to go to his mami and clutch her hand before he took the small dais but hadn't expected to find her in what sounded like an argument.

"Mira, Juana, no había un hombre—understand?" Alma said, waving a finger playfully at the other woman, who was looking down and shaking her head. "I remember everyone that was there, and this just—no pasó así, ¿entiendes? When Pedro was—when they took him from me, it was los conquistadores, me, and my—"

She stopped abruptly once she noticed Bruno approaching.

"Oh, Bruno, you remember Juana Mazorra, right?" Alma said, pointing at the woman, who seemed sheepish upon recognizing Bruno. "She's one of the oldest residents of Encanto. I've known her almost my whole life."

"Wow, that's amazing," Bruno said, still processing what he'd heard—wondering if he'd heard anything, really. "What's going on?"

"Oh, nada, mijo. Tú sabes—hablando," Alma said with a playful shrug. "Are you coming up to talk next, mi niño? Qué bello fue lo que dicieron tus hermanas, ¿no?"

Bruno nodded.

"Yes, I'm heading up, but I wanted—"

Before Bruno could finish, the loud, melodic strum of the band's bandola llanera seemed to cut through the cold night air. A voice boomed over the entire gathering.

"Let's have some music, shall we?" the bandleader yelled as his bandmates took the stage that Bruno had been heading toward. He tried to keep his shoulders from sagging. He felt his mother's hands on his arm.

"Ay, Bruno, tell them you want to talk," she said, her face close to his. "I want to hear what you have to say."

Bruno gave her a sideways hug and stepped away slowly.

"It's fine, Mami," he said, trying to keep that practiced smile on his face—the forced, joyous expression he'd been practicing for weeks. "I want you to enjoy the music."

She didn't respond. She was back to talking to Juana, the debate becoming more heated. The next thing Bruno knew, he was on the makeshift dance floor, trying his best to keep up with the music. He scanned everyone around him—taking in the smiles, the laughter, the rhythm—and a familiar feeling overwhelmed him. A sense of otherness. A sense of being outside of something common and universal. A sense that what he was feeling was somehow too different for this place.

Bruno Madrigal, surrounded by the people of Encanto, enveloped in love and joy, had never, ever felt so alone.

And it broke his heart.

CHAPTER
TWENTY-FOUR

He had to lean into it.

That was the big thought in Bruno's mind as he watched the party wind down. Watched the various residents of Encanto approaching his mami and thanking her for everything—her work, her kindness, her generosity. He felt like a ghost as he looked at Julieta and Pepa standing near Alma, like her faithful attendants. Did they even need him? he wondered.

He thought back to Pepa's visit, when she'd brought up the goldfish and how Bruno's vision had been wrong. He hadn't truly considered the consequences of his actions, that perhaps telling people exactly what they wanted to hear might be more problematic in the long run. But what could he do about it now? He slid a hand over his hair, tied back in a tight bun. He looked down at the silk shirt and tailored slacks he wore. He looked nice. Or he looked like what he thought nice should look like. Roberto had helped him pick out the clothes, styled his hair. He'd even given Bruno tips on how to walk, how to maintain eye contact, when to laugh and smile. It had worked, Bruno told himself. He was approachable now. People sought him out and were excited to see him. Even tonight, as low as Bruno felt, he had been surrounded by people. Girls and boys danced with and around him. He felt eyes on him. Why didn't it feel good, though?

"I must be doing something wrong," he said to himself.

"What could it be?"

Bruno turned to see Roberto standing next to him, a wide grin on his face. He looked nice, too, but also comfortable—not like Bruno, an alien in his own skin. Trapped by his own behaviors. He felt a surge of relief as he hugged his friend. His only true friend, really.

"You still shaken up about your sisters?" Roberto asked, looking toward Alma and her daughters.

"Don't let it get to you. They don't understand what you're doing."

Bruno nodded. He appreciated Roberto's support. The more he thought about it, the more it seemed like Roberto was the only person in Encanto who did support him. Alma, Julieta, and Pepa loved him—in their way. They cared. But did they understand what Bruno was dealing with? What Bruno was trying to do? When he had attempted to explain his vision of betrayal to his mami, she'd danced around it, more worried about Encanto and the magic now, not in the future.

Perhaps that is a clue unto itself.

The thought popped into Bruno's brain like a flashing light.

What could it mean?

"It's hard to not let it get to me," Bruno said in a low voice so only Roberto could hear. He was still putting on the smile, showing his public face for those milling about. But he really felt like he wanted to run up to his room, shut off the lights, and curl up in his tiny bed forever. He wanted to feel the blackness, the void, and come out when he was ready to see the world—if ever. "I know they care about me, but they don't want to know about me, ¿sabes? They don't want to think about why I'm doing anything. They're just annoyed by it. 'Bruno, Mami is worried.' Is she worried about me, though? Or is she worried about what it might mean for Encanto—or how it might reflect on her?"

Bruno looked at Roberto, who seemed taken aback by his complaint. Had he pushed it too far? he wondered.

"It's normal to feel that way," Roberto said, frowning slightly. "I know your sisters love you, Bruno. But love doesn't always mean acceptance or understanding."

Bruno stepped toward Roberto.

"You know what I mean?" Bruno asked. He felt a rush of affection for Roberto. The understanding his friend had shared had landed at the right time. The perfect time, really. Maybe he wasn't alone.

"Of course I do," Roberto said with a grin. "You're not the only outcast in Encanto, Bruno Madrigal. But there's a solution, I think."

"I think so, too," Bruno said, looking toward Casita. He watched as neighbors and residents helped move tables and trays back inside the house.

I should lend a hand, too, he thought. "I think I need to help this place. I need to do what I feel is right."

"Which is?"

Bruno swallowed hard. He wasn't sure he should say anything, had thought he wouldn't—but Roberto's friendship felt so true, and so needed. He wanted to have someone to confide in.

"You know this, Roberto . . . but it haunts me, what I saw . . . something terrible," Bruno said. "I sensed that someone would betray me, and betray Encanto. That the magic would be destroyed. I need to do whatever I can to prevent that. But I have no idea who might want to hurt us. Hurt my family. And what if . . . ?"

His voice trailed off. Roberto's eyes narrowed.

"What if . . . what?"

"What if the people betraying Encanto . . . betraying me . . ." Bruno said. "What if it's my own family? What if they don't mean to—but they make a mistake? What if, in their desire to preserve every-thing the way it is, they destroy its future?"

CHAPTER
TWENTY-FIVE

The vision struck Bruno down later that night as he sat on his bed. His room was pitch-black, the only illumination coming from his tiny window—a thin shaft of moonlight sneaking in. It'd been hours since the party ended, but Bruno couldn't sleep. He felt the weight of his realization and it chilled him to the bone. He couldn't believe it, but he also trusted his gut—his gift. Someone was going to betray him, and it was starting to look like it might be his own—

His entire body froze. A swirl of smoky green light spun around his head as a vision formed in front of his eyes—sudden, jarring, lifelike. He heard himself cry out, but even that sounded distant and muted—as if he were listening through a window.

He saw himself, standing before Casita—watching as someone, a dark, looming figure, stood before the house, waving their arms. Strange energies pulsed from the figure's hands. He saw his family—Julieta, Pepa, Alma—bowing down before the figure. Worshipping them? Bruno gasped and saw two more figures in the foreground looking on in a panic—desperate to stop whatever was happening. He wanted to scream, to reach out, but he couldn't. But somehow his yelps of surprise cut through the vision, and Bruno saw one of the people turn to him—and once again, Bruno saw himself. But it wasn't the frightening older version of Bruno he'd seen earlier. It was him now, looking shaken and disheveled but still wearing his new clothes and new hairstyle.

"We've been betrayed—everything is lost," dream Bruno said to the figure next to him, draped in shadow. Bruno could tell this was a friend—a confidant. But what was happening? Why was his family bowing down before this cloaked figure? Who could they be?

Bruno tried to reach into the vision again, squinting his eyes to get a better look at what was happening, but as soon as he did, it began to dissolve—becoming that strange green smoke. He gasped. He could still feel it, what he'd seen, as if he were there—and he would be there. Much sooner than he'd anticipated. When he'd had that traumatic vision—of himself in the crawl spaces of the house, alone, scraggly, and unhinged—it had felt so far away. The distance had dulled the shock to some degree. It would take time to get there. But this moment—this vision that foretold the very end of Encanto and Casita—could happen as soon as tomorrow, it seemed like.

He was shaking. His mouth was dry. Even though he was sitting in a pitch-black room, Bruno's eyes darted around, looking for movement, for anything—a sign, a sense that things would be okay. That what he'd seen was a nightmare, not a vision. Not something that could ever come true.

"I have to think," he said to himself as he jumped to his feet and began to pace around. "I have to figure out what to do."

He thought back to the vision, still fresh in his mind. The mysterious villain at the center. His family bowing at their feet. Bruno and an unknown ally trying to save the town, to save Casita and the Encanto. It had become clearer to Bruno—he had two visions to prevent, two dark futures to avoid. One predicted where Bruno would end up, and another, more widespread one promised a betrayal that could hurt all of Encanto. Were they the same? It'd seemed so clear to him earlier. To avoid becoming the isolated pariah he first saw, he had to become someone else—someone brighter, happier, more *social*, and *friendlier*. Bruno believed it had worked so far. But what if that wasn't enough? What if he wasn't trying hard enough to change who he really was?

"Could this be my fault?"

The words hung in the air, spreading over the darkened room like the thick green smoke of his vision. What if his attempts to become someone else helped in some ways but hurt in others? His mind was spinning out. Anxiety was spreading over him. His thoughts ping-ponged in his head—every thread, every idea, every situation catapulting beyond the real and concrete to the darkest, most dangerous worst-case scenario.

After some time, Bruno realized it was almost morning. His head ached. He hadn't figured out what to do next. But he had figured something else out. And he knew who he had to talk to about

it. Someone he should have spoken to long ago—
someone he should have confided in once the visions
about Casita had started.

Bruno took a deep breath and began to dress
himself, trying meticulously to maintain the
appearance and vibe he'd so carefully crafted over
the past few weeks. Losing that, he knew, wouldn't
help. He had to stave off his own dark future if he
had any chance of helping Encanto.

He was alone now, he realized. He couldn't trust
anyone—because his visions gave him no leads, no
answers.

It was all up to him.

CHAPTER
TWENTY-SIX

"**L**ookin' sharp, Bruno."

It took a second for Bruno to register the words, much less where they were coming from. He'd been so deep in his own thoughts. He turned around to find Annalise walking toward him, a toothy smile on her face.

"Where are you headed?"

"Oh, not sure—just needed to get some fresh air, you know," he said with a smile, reminding himself to stay in character—to stay close to this new, better version of himself. "Great to see you, though."

"It really is amazing," Annalise said, keeping pace with Bruno as they walked toward the town's more residential stretch—a quieter, more cramped part of Encanto. "What you've done, you know? Everyone feels so much lighter now. Ever since the town was created—from what my mami and papi tell me—there was this sense of fear. Of anxiety. That it would all . . . I dunno, go away, or change into something else. But now everyone seems a little more optimistic. A little more invincible."

Bruno winced in response but pushed back. He didn't think Annalise had noticed the fleeting change. Why had he responded that way?

"Thank you," Bruno said, nodding and smiling at Annalise. "I appreciate that. I want people to feel safe here. To understand that the future isn't scary. It's a gift."

Annalise frowned, a quick expression that faded in a moment.

"Do you really think that?" she asked.

Bruno, still wearing his friendliest smile, nodded.

"Of course I do," he said. "I have this gift—this special tool. Why not use it to help everyone around me?"

Annalise didn't respond right away, instead looking down the narrow alley they were walking through, seeming lost in thought.

"I'm grateful for what you've done," she said, not meeting his eyes. "It's really helped a lot of people during a tough time, I think. I just—I just wanted to say thank you. And to, well, commend you on your fashion sense once more."

Bruno's spirits rose. Why couldn't everyone be like this? Supportive, kind, understanding? He needed this, he realized. After years of trying to just get by—sidestepping the land mines of his own anxiety to get through the day—he was doing something different. He wished the people he cared about noticed it. No, that wasn't the problem. He wished they *appreciated* him for it.

Annalise continued. Bruno tried to soak up this moment, her familiar tone, the warmth between them. He wanted to be here forever. It was comfortable to not be judged or criticized, to just be able to walk and enjoy someone else's company, without worrying about gifts, visions, or the future.

"I bet you're excited for your sister, huh?" Annalise asked, nudging him with her elbow.

"Sister? What do you mean?"

"Oh, Julieta—I'm sure you heard, right?" Annalise said. "Everyone is talking about it, Bruno."

He started to respond to Annalise, but something caught his eye—something moving in the distance behind her. A figure. He felt a flash of recognition. A sense that not only had he seen this person before, but *he knew them*. He looked up and watched as the shadowy figure made their way toward him. Bruno's blood ran cold.

CHAPTER
TWENTY-SEVEN

The anxiety spike was sharp. Suddenly Bruno felt a lightness in his head, slick sweat over his palms. He could feel his heart thumping, struggling to burst out of his chest. The figure was gone, but he knew he'd seen it. Seen *him*. The dark, mysterious presence from his vision. The person behind it all. The figure who would manipulate everyone—anyone—against him.

"Bruno, are you . . . are you okay?" Annalise asked, grabbing his arm. "You look so pale suddenly—¿qué te pasa? Did I upset you?"

Bruno pulled away and took a few hesitant steps backward—his eyes still locked on the place where he'd seen the shadowy figure. It had been heading toward him, Bruno thought. He was certain. Things were moving too fast. The visions. His realizations.

Bruno clutched his head. He felt helpless and powerless. What could he do now? Now that this shadow-creature was here, in Encanto, hunting him down?

He turned from Annalise and walked quickly in the opposite direction from where he'd seen the shadowy figure. He needed help. But who could help him now?

He picked up the pace, darting past the grocery and through a small park. With every few steps, Bruno allowed himself a glance back. Each time, there was nothing. No shadow lurking after him. No green smoke. Nothing. But still he walked on. He needed to talk to someone. *Where is Roberto when I need him?* Bruno thought. He just wanted to think aloud—to have someone tell him, "No, Bruno, you're fine. You haven't lost your mind. This is totally normal and totally okay. You will be okay."

Who could tell him that now?

Bruno realized he'd stopped walking. He was on his knees near a few bushes at the far end of the field adjacent to the park. His hands were covering his face. His eyes were wet. Had he blacked out? How long had he been here, crying by himself? He wiped at his face and had started to get up when he felt a strong hand on his shoulder. He heard a familiar low, rumbling voice before he could turn to see who it was.

"Bruno Madrigal—¿qué haces?"

CHAPTER
TWENTY-EIGHT

"I don't want to talk about Bruno, Mami."

Pepa's words seemed to hover over the kitchen in Casita, where Julieta and Alma also stood. The mood was sharp—everyone on edge, milling about and redoing things that had been done hours before, just to keep their hands busy. Alma had summoned her two daughters to the kitchen to catch up. Part of her was still floating—celebrating the momentous party her children and her neighbors had thrown for her the night before. But also, she wanted to address something else. Something that she now realized she could not fix on her own.

Bruno.

"Bueno, we have to, Pepa," Alma said, wiping off an already dry bowl and placing it back on the drying rack. "Something is bothering him. You've both tried to speak to him, I've tried to speak to him—y nada. He is set on this journey for himself. He wants to . . . become someone else."

"And would that be so bad?" Pepa asked with a shrug. "I mean, I thought it was weird, too, but now the more I think about it—well, fine! Fine, Bruno— stop being so weird. Is that a problem? That he smiles at people? Hangs out? Tries to be normal?"

Alma watched Julieta react, watched her nose scrunch up and her mouth form a frown.

"Pepa, what in the world is normal?" Julieta said sharply. "You're just mad about your wedding— still. Just move on. Bruno is who he is. What worries me is that he's not happy with that, and he's forcing himself to be what he thinks *we* want him to be."

Pepa folded her arms and turned to her mother, ignoring Julieta.

"It can't just be Bruno, Mami, because we've always been worried about him," she said calmly. "Is there something else? You seem almost frantic this morning."

"Yeah, what is it, Mami?" Julieta said, joining her sister in a chorus of concern. "What can we do to help? Is everything fine? Are you sick?"

Alma shook her head solemnly.

"No, mis niñas, it is not me—it's . . . everything else," she said, looking up at the ceiling. "I feel— I feel like something is wrong, something is off. No lo puedo explicar—but something is disrupting my connection. To Encanto, to the magic—everything. And it's only going to get worse."

Pepa and Julieta both audibly gasped.

"What do you mean, Mami? It's Bruno, isn't it? He's messing with his gift and it's going to ruin everything for—"

"No sé, Pepa. I do not know," Alma continued. "That might be part of it. But I feel he is doing this for a reason—and it might be part of a bigger problem."

Alma thought back to the night before, to watching Bruno—the false smile on his face, the awkward movements. She could tell that inside, her baby was suffering. He was in pain. Why hadn't she noticed it sooner? she wondered. She felt a great weight of guilt on her shoulders—and a looming sense that there was very little she could do to fix it.

"Someone is trying to twist the magic—this special gift we all have with Encanto—to do what they want," Alma said gravely. "I can feel it. I can feel the magic being disrupted, contorted. But I can't put my finger on who—or why. Not fully."

She thought back to another part of the evening—to her lively conversation with her friend Juana Mazorra. They'd known each other since the first days of Encanto. Had kept no secrets from each other. Juana was chatty and circuitous in how she spoke. It was easy to lose the narrative. But last night she'd seemed hyperfocused on a story Alma had told her years ago, just a few short days after Encanto was formed. About someone with them—on that night. The night Pedro died. Another person who'd witnessed it all. But was that even possible? Alma chided herself for not listening—not paying attention to the details Juana had shared, but Alma couldn't hear over the din of the party. Something about this felt important, and Alma felt like she was grasping at a puff of smoke right in front of her eyes.

Julieta pulled Alma out of her reverie.

"But you have an idea, don't you?" Julieta asked.

Alma took in a sharp breath. Julieta knew her too well—could read her mind, almost.

"All I know, all I sense, is that what is coming is somehow tied to our dear Bruno," Alma said, choosing her words carefully. "I worry it's that cloaked man, Francisco. He seems to be interested in Bruno and the history of the town. He seems to have always been around us, but never clear to me. But it could be someone else. Someone we trust who we do not fully understand, who weaves into our lives in unexpected ways. I shudder to think it could be someone who lives here, in this place we've built, but it's possible. I feel an imbalance in the world around us. The energies that flow through me, through this village, están mal. They feel off, bad. I've never felt anything like it, and I hope we can fix it. Soon. I wish I had more to share, my daughters. I wish I knew what to do next."

Alma covered her face. She fought back the tears she knew were forming. She hated showing any weakness—especially hated doing it in front of her children. She felt Julieta and Pepa embrace her from either side.

"It's okay, Mami," Julieta whispered. "We're here."

"We have to protect Encanto," Alma said, refusing to weep. "We must do whatever it takes. Do you understand?"

"Of course, Mami," Pepa said.

Julieta pulled away slowly.

"I'll do whatever we need to do, you both know that," Julieta said. "But we need to be careful with Bruno. He's our brother. We love him. He's struggling and we need to be there for him, not push him away. Whoever or whatever is trying to manipulate Encanto and the energies that reside here is zeroing in on him—but why? That's what I want to know. And I want to protect him."

Alma and her two daughters linked hands.

"We have to protect both," Alma said, looking at her daughters, her eyes wet with tears. "Because if we succeed with one but lose the other, we've lost forever."

CHAPTER
TWENTY-NINE

"Are you worried?"

Pepa's question hit Julieta seconds after they'd finished ushering their mami upstairs to rest, just as they began their descent to the first floor.

"Worried? Of course," Julieta said, not looking up at her sister, a few steps behind her in the stairwell. "Mami knows Encanto better than any of us. If she senses something is off, something is off—and that's not good."

"This is Bruno's fault," Pepa said flatly. "I don't think he's doing it on purpose, of course, but if he wasn't messing around with his gift, we wouldn't be—"

"Pepa, cállate por un momento, por Dios," Julieta said sternly. "Stop and think for a second. Bruno is not like us. He's different. But that's okay. You know that. We have to show Bruno we love him no matter what—no matter what he looks like, acts like, or does. He's a Madrigal and he has a gift. It's a more challenging gift than ours. I cook and make people happy. You can control the weather. He sees what's coming—good or bad. Can you blame him for wanting to change that?"

"I don't know, Julieta."

"Think of it this way," Julieta said. "Imagine your wedding day—what if Bruno had walked in and said, 'It's going to be a perfect day, not a cloud in the sky.' How would you have reacted?"

"I would've been relieved," Pepa said with a shrug. "So what?"

"But that's not Bruno," Julieta said, placing her hands on her sister's arms. "He doesn't have the ability to just lie like that. It's not him. But you would have felt better, no? You would have been glad?"

"But . . . but then it would have rained anyway," Pepa said, her eyes distant as she realized something she hadn't considered before.

"Right," Julieta said. "So how would you have

felt then? If you'd realized Bruno had *lied* to you? Or tried to cover up the truth to protect you?"

Pepa frowned.

"I—I don't know," she said. "I guess I would have been upset. Or appreciative of him trying to make me feel better? It's complicated."

Julieta pulled her sister in for a tight hug.

"Exactly, hermanita," she said. "It's not easy. Bruno is having a hard time. That's my main concern. We have to help him."

Pepa nodded in agreement. Julieta had opened her mouth to let Pepa know she was going to find Bruno when Pepa spoke.

"Before you run off to be the hero, hermanita— what are you going to do about Roberto?"

"What do you mean?"

"Mami told me—she was telling everyone last night," Pepa said with a knowing smile. "About his proposal."

Julieta blushed. She hated herself for that but couldn't help the reaction. She stopped on her way to the door and turned to her sister.

"He did," she said. "I told him—well, I said no. I don't think it's a good fit. I kept it a little vague, because, well—I'm not sure. But it was still no. I guess I just didn't want to hurt his feelings."

"Are you worried about how people might react?" Pepa asked. "It feels like the entire village was buzzing about Roberto proposing."

Julieta sighed.

"That's part of it," she said. "I felt a lot of pressure. People were asking me about it before I even saw Roberto, before he even got on his knee and asked me to marry him. I didn't want that. I didn't want to feel like I was letting people down."

"Like Bruno?" Pepa asked.

Julieta nodded.

"Yes," she said. "I know he loves Roberto. That they're close. He wants him to be in our family, and I think—maybe—he would be great. But I'm just . . . I'm just not sure. I'm so indecisive. It feels like too big a decision to shrug off. I'm just not sure, Pepa."

"What's not to be sure about, sis?" Pepa said. "Roberto is smart, funny, handsome, and loves you and our family. He even loves hanging out with Bruno. He's perfect."

Julieta looked down at her hands.

"He's almost . . . too perfect," Julieta said. "Every-one who's courted me—Hernán, Agustín, that Peña boy . . . they were all great but also had flaws. Like real people. A short temper. A daydreamer. A close talker. Big things, little things. We all have them. But I've never heard anything cross about Roberto. It's like he was carved from stone and given life."

Julieta laughed at her description.

"It's just hard to think of his flaws," Julieta said. "Maybe he doesn't have any."

"Too perfect, Julieta? There's no such thing," Pepa said, draping an arm over her sister's shoulder as they walked out to the foyer. "Trust me on this."

"He is very handsome . . ." Julieta said, her voice trailing off.

"See, there you go," Pepa said with a laugh. "It's not that hard to envision you two together, exchang-ing vows. Maybe give him another chance?"

Julieta stepped away from her sister and stood in the doorway to Casita. She looked out on the town, watching the bustling crowd and listening to the sounds of Encanto.

"But what if there's someone else? What about . . .

I dunno," Julieta said. "What about someone like Agustín?"

Pepa let out a long laugh.

"Agustín? No digas locuras, Julieta," she said. "Agustín is nice, I guess, but he's kind of strange—and so clumsy and awkward. How many times have you had to cook something to help him recover from this injury or that? He's a mess. Meanwhile, Roberto is smooth as silk."

Julieta sighed.

"Mami doesn't think Agustín deserves me," she said, looking down at her feet. "But he is sweet. And I feel like he has a good heart. That's something you can just sense. And I don't mind growing alongside him—both of us learning how to be together."

"Now you're just talking in riddles," Pepa said, turning away.

Julieta followed her sister back into the house.

"It's not a riddle, Pepa," she said. "Roberto is almost too perfect. I wonder what happens when things get tough. Is that the person who will be there then, too? I don't know. He seems perfectly nice and charming. But with Agustín—he is loyal and kind. A gentle soul. I'm just . . . I'm just not ready to decide."

Pepa placed a hand on Julieta's cheek.

"Decide with your heart," she said. "What is it that you want?"

Julieta thought for a second, then looked at her sister.

"I want someone true," she said. "True to me— true to Encanto, and, most important . . . true to themself."

Excerpt from Julieta Madrigal's Diary

Everyone is on edge. It feels like Encanto is coming apart, slowly, at the seams. I'm struggling, diary. I'm feeling pressure from all sides. From Roberto, Mami, Bruno—myself. Even Pepa. I wish I could just think about the little things—about who will take me out or who I can invite to meet my family. But I also know something else is happening. Something dangerous.

And how is Bruno? What about all the things he's telling people? Are they true? Is he making it worse by lying? What's driven him to take these liberties? I worry about him, dear diary. So much.

Pepa told me that she's worried about how Bruno will take the news of me rejecting Roberto's proposal. I'm worried, too. It feels like the worst possible time to surprise Bruno. He seems so unsteady these days. And then I go back to wondering about our village. About the people of the Encanto. What is happening to us?

Mami knows. She knows what's happening—and I think she knows why.

I pray we all find out in time to save ourselves. To save Encanto.

I pray for Bruno, too.

CHAPTER
THIRTY

"**Y**ou look like you've seen a ghost, Bruno."

Bruno glanced up to see who was speaking and could barely contain his relief. It was Agustín, a teen about his own age who had a towering crush on Julieta. Everyone knew except, perhaps, Julieta herself.

Agustín struck Bruno as a kind person—friendly, personable, and thoughtful—if a bit awkward and clumsy. There wasn't a bucket in the town that Agustín hadn't stepped in, or a rope he hadn't tripped on. But he had a good heart, Bruno thought, and this was another sign of that. Whatever he'd seen had driven Agustín to follow Bruno to the clearing, to check on him. And that was worth something.

"Oh, I, uh—I'm fine," Bruno said, standing up and wiping at his face. He tried to recover and reconstitute the new Bruno—the smile, the wit, the demeanor. But he was having trouble. He felt an ache inside himself he couldn't pinpoint, something preventing him in this moment from trying to be anything but his true self.

"Well, that's good," Agustín said, watching Bruno warily. "Because you looked completely terrified. Annalise said you just ran off in a panic."

Bruno waved it off.

"Oh, it wasn't like that," he said. "I thought I'd forgotten something at home, so I bolted."

"But, Bruno," Agustín said, following Bruno as he walked back the way he'd come, "your house is in the other direction."

Bruno let out a humorless laugh.

"I guess . . . I guess you're right, Agustín," Bruno said. He sighed and looked at the other teen, sizing him up slowly. His expression was open, a look of genuine concern on his face. Bruno felt a warmth toward him he couldn't explain, a feeling of familiarity and friendship, as if they'd known each other for years. "I'm just not feeling like myself lately."

Agustín nodded, though it was clear he didn't

fully understand what Bruno meant. The two walked back together, toward Casita.

"It's hard to even figure out who you are sometimes," Agustín said, his eyes on the path, perhaps for fear of tripping, Bruno guessed. "I know I struggle with it. I think we're at that age, Bruno, where we're trying to boil down who we are—and who we're going to be. But there's no guarantee we're getting it right."

Bruno didn't respond. He wasn't sure what to say. He was just happy for a peaceful moment—even if it was with someone he barely knew. He felt slight embarrassment, too, for having Agustín find him in such disarray. But he appreciated how Agustín just shrugged it off. Agustín continued to talk, unfazed by Bruno's silence.

"I think about it a lot, too, because you want to fit in. I know I do," he said, kicking a rock and slipping slightly. Bruno leaned in to support him, avoiding disaster. After a quick thanks, Agustín continued. "I'm sure you know this, but I—uh— I really like your sister Julieta. She's wonderful. The most beautiful girl I've ever seen. Inside and out.

Kind, generous, and humble. From the moment I saw her, I knew I wanted to be with her as much as I could. But I also know I'm not the kind of person who should be asking for her hand, or trying to be with her. Someone charming, handsome, and dashing—that's what she should have. Why would she spend her time with someone like me?"

"Don't be so hard on yourself," Bruno said.

"That's the thing, though," Agustín continued. "We are harder on ourselves than anyone else, Bruno. You say 'Don't be so hard on yourself' with such ease—but do you give yourself that same grace? I mean, we don't know each other well—but I have seen you. I've seen you trying to move around town and make people happy, trying to change how you look and act. It must be so hard. I've wondered if I could ever do that—if I would ever do that—to win Julieta's hand. But my answer is no."

"No?" Bruno asked. "Even for Julieta?"

They'd reached a small clearing near the hustle and bustle of Encanto's town square. Bruno could hear the rhythms of the town growing louder as they approached.

"If I'm not enough for Julieta—me, and my

strengths and my faults," Agustín said, looking at Bruno, a sheepish smile on his face, "then it's just not meant to be. I can't change myself to be something I'm not. I'm happy with who I am. I love myself. If someone else can't see how great I am, then it's okay—I don't want to be with someone who doesn't want to be with me. And I think you're great, too, Bruno."

Agustín shook Bruno's hand.

"You deserve to be happy. And the best way to be happy is to realize who you are—and what you want to do," Agustín said. "Being yourself comes naturally, Bruno. It's not a muscle you have to activate or a script you need to read. I think, in your heart, you know that, too."

Bruno nodded.

"I do," he said.

"Then there's your—"

Agustín's words were drowned out by something—someone—else. Bruno heard his name being yelled from farther in the town. Then he saw a familiar shape running toward him, looking fit and heroic. Roberto.

"Bruno, where've you been?" Roberto said,

stopping in front of him and Agustín. "I've been looking all over for you."

Roberto looked at Agustín as if he were just noticing him.

"Oh, Agustín, hi," he said.

Agustín nodded in response.

Roberto turned his attention back to Bruno.

"I guess you've heard," Roberto said flatly, clearly trying to watch his words around Agustín.

Bruno shrugged in confusion.

"About?"

"Your sister," Roberto said, his words sharp. He looked at Agustín. "I'm sure you're quite happy."

Agustín didn't move, his eyes on Roberto.

"Julieta is her own woman," Agustín said. "She can choose who she wants."

Roberto scoffed. "As long as it's you, right?" Roberto turned his attention back to Bruno, scanning him from head to toe. "Bruno, what happened to you?"

"What do you mean?" Bruno asked.

"Your shirt is torn," Roberto said, running a finger over a slight rip. "And you look like you've been rolling in the dirt. You don't want to look like that in town. You need to change. Straighten up your hair. And smile! Be happy! That's what people want, Bruno."

"Is it?" Agustín asked, looking at Roberto.

Roberto turned to face Agustín, his eyes narrowed.

"What do you mean? Bruno has figured out what he wants to do," he said. Roberto glanced at Bruno. "Isn't that right?"

Bruno started to respond but couldn't find the words.

Roberto motioned for Bruno to follow him. As the two wandered a few feet away from Agustín, Roberto turned to him.

"I know what I'm talking about," he said. "It's worked for me. And it was working for you. But you have to be consistent, Bruno. People don't want to be around someone strange and unsettling—someone who might know something bad about them. They want to be around someone fun, charming, and easygoing. You might want to take my advice, too, Agustín—it might help you in your own life, no?"

"Very funny, Roberto," Agustín called to them. "You're quite the clown."

Bruno turned back to look at Agustín as they walked away, toward Casita. He saw his new friend's expression change, from calm to something closer to anger. It made Bruno feel unsettled. Did he truly know Agustín Espinoza all that well? Could he trust him? Bruno wasn't sure. He turned away from him and walked with Roberto, wondering about Encanto and how much of his vision was on its way to becoming a dangerous reality.

CHAPTER
THIRTY-ONE

Alma Madrigal watched as the dusk settled over Encanto. She felt a soft breeze hit her face as she rocked in the worn wooden chair on the front porch of La Casa Madrigal. Any other time, this would have been the height of relaxation for Alma—a moment to mull over the day and look toward a good, hearty sleep. But she couldn't relax. Even after her conversation with Julieta and Pepa, she still felt on edge.

She'd worked so hard—tirelessly—for years to help build this place, this haven, for her family and for the residents of Encanto. From the darkest tragedy, the death of her beloved Pedro, some hope had sprung. Or so she'd thought. But what if she'd only managed to stave off darkness for a while—and it was looming over her and her family yet again? The thought worried Alma Madrigal.

There was someone else there, *Alma. You told me so—don't you remember?*

Juana Mazorra's words echoed in Alma's mind, and there was nothing she could do to shake them away. She had no recollection of telling Juana this— and she wasn't getting so on in years that she was having full-on memory lapses, Alma thought. But then why did Juana's story sound so familiar? The faded memory, clouded by the darkness and tragedy of Pedro's death and fleeing with her children . . . Had Alma seen something else? She thought back to that night, to their escape from the conquistadores—and then she saw it. For the first time—but for the millionth time, it felt like—a cloaked figure, wandering behind them, lurking like a vulture circling its prey. Had Alma imagined this just now—or had her conversation with Juana unlocked something deep inside her mind? Something she'd hidden or . . .

Alma gasped.

Something that had been hidden from her.

She got up quickly, her mind racing. The evil—the

betrayal—hovering over her, over everyone, was moving faster than she could have imagined. It was rooted in the town's earliest days. It was not something heading toward Encanto—

It was already here.

She had to talk to Bruno. She needed him to clear his mind, to use his gift—to see what was coming. But was it too late? Already her son's gift had been diluted and twisted, his connection to it frayed and clouded. That put them all at risk, Alma knew. They'd taken him—and his gift—for granted, always assuming it'd be there, that Bruno would always be welcoming and helpful. But something was interfering with that—making it not only harder for them to reach Bruno but harder for Bruno to truly see what was next. It was creating a cloud of confusion and uncertainty that worried Alma more than she could admit. They'd all been in denial, Alma realized—and they had to face the problem if they wanted any chance of saving Encanto.

"It's him," she muttered to herself as she grabbed her jacket and turned back to the front door. She needed to find Bruno. But she also knew who might be behind it all. "Francisco. I should have known. I should have seen it."

As the door creaked shut behind her, Alma hurried down Casita's front steps, not looking ahead of her until it was almost too late.

The cloaked man seemed to be running toward the house at full speed, his tattered covering fluttering behind him. Alma knew she couldn't escape. She whispered a prayer and waited.

CHAPTER
THIRTY-TWO

"**W**hy do you seem so down, Bruno? You should be happy. You're doing exactly what you set out to do."

Bruno didn't look up in response to Roberto, who seemed to be running next to and around him as Bruno lumbered through Encanto's backstreets.

"You're getting the reaction you always wanted, no?" Roberto asked, almost pleading. "Everyone I talk to is so glad—you're giving them the joy they were desperate for."

Bruno gripped his head and spun around to face Roberto.

"But it's not real," he said, raising his voice. "It's a guess. It's a fabrication. I'm telling people what I think they want to hear, and I'm trying to make sure it feels believable—not too outlandish, not too sweet and forced—but it's not a vision, Roberto. It's not something I see."

Bruno tapped the side of his head.

"Those visions are different," Bruno continued. "I can't control them. I can't change them. They are what they are, good or bad. I can't help it. So, when someone would ask me, before, I'd tell them—good or bad. It made me a freak. A shadow. The person people feared—because maybe Bruno would have bad news for them today. Maybe he would see something terrible, something dark. And sometimes I did."

Bruno sat on the ground. He leaned forward, folding into himself, his head between his knees. He wasn't even sure if Roberto was still around. He didn't care. He just needed to vent.

"I'm a fraud. . . ."

His voice was a croak, an empty, broken sound emanating from his mouth. He heard shuffling and looked up. Roberto was still there, looking down at Bruno. He extended a hand and helped him to his feet.

"You're not a fraud," Roberto said. "You're my friend. And you're just trying to be the best you can be. You're just trying to be helpful to others. What's the harm in that?"

"The harm is, he's lying."

Bruno and Roberto looked back down the alley and saw Agustín, less than a yard away. How much had he heard? Bruno wondered. Did it matter?

"Agustín—where were you?" Bruno asked, alarmed at how the teen had seemingly appeared out of nowhere, and he was reminded of the angry expression on Agustín's face just a bit earlier.

"I was doing research," Agustín said, shifting his weight from one foot to the other, his eyes on Roberto. "I spoke to an old friend about you, Roberto. We realized we have the same perspective about what Bruno is doing—and how much of it is your fault."

"What are you talking about?" Roberto said, stepping toward Agustín.

"He's giving people false hope—and in the process, he's distancing himself from who he really is," Agustín said, his voice calm and gentle, like it always was. Bruno watched Agustín stumble slightly as he walked over to them, never losing his focus. "His intentions were good, of course, but life is hard—life is about loss and struggle and tragedy mixed with joy and hope. It's never just one or the other. I think in the process of, well, trying to do some good in Encanto, Bruno—you might be doing harm."

Bruno looked at Roberto and saw his friend bristle. His back tensed. His smile flattened into a stoic sneer. Bruno had never seen him like this. It worried him.

"Bruno is doing the right thing," Roberto said, standing right in front of Agustín, who refused to back away. "You don't know what he's dealing with. You're not his friend. You're just another guy pining for his sister."

"I could say the same for you, Roberto," Agustín said with a shrug. "I'm not trying to win anything. If Bruno wants to listen to what I have to say, that's good. If not, I can't make him. I'm not sure that's your perspective, though."

"What is that supposed to mean?" Roberto spat.

Bruno stepped forward, trying to get between Roberto and Agustín, but they were interrupted by something else.

They all heard the footsteps at the same time. Not one pair, not two—but a crowd. At least ten or fifteen people stomping toward them. Bruno recognized many of the townspeople as they approached. He'd seen most of them just last night, celebrating his mami's birthday. It'd been a joyous, wonderful night. One Bruno would never forget.

But something told him he would never forget this night, either, Bruno thought.

"What's going on?" Bruno said to the crowd of neighbors, who all seemed to be focused on him. The small group formed a half circle around him, Roberto, and Agustín. "What is this?"

He recognized the person who stepped forward immediately, and he already knew what Señora Anta was going to say.

"He's gone," the older woman said, her words coming out in a choked sob. She was clutching a hat—a faded fedora that Bruno recognized as Julio's. His heart broke. "He died, Bruno. My Julio. He was doing so much better—just like you said. Like you foretold. He was laughing, talking, even helping around the house. Then yesterday . . . he just withered away. It was like his illness came back even stronger than before. Dios mío . . . I don't know what I'll do without him. . . ."

Bruno stepped forward as the woman's voice trailed off.

"I'm . . . I'm so sorry, Señora Anta," he said, his voice quivering. He felt unmoored. What could he do to comfort this woman who had lost everything? He thought he heard Agustín gasp behind him. "Julio was a good man. . . ."

"Then why did you lie?"

Another voice. Bruno looked over Señora Anta's shoulders to see Antonia, one of the many people he'd spoken to over the past week or so. Her concern had been different—minor, if he was being honest, especially in comparison to Señora Anta's. She'd been worried she'd failed a test, and Bruno had—again, trying to be helpful—assured her she'd passed.

"You told me I passed that test, Bruno," Antonia said, her face a scowl. "And I failed. Failed so badly that my teacher took me aside and told me I was maybe getting kicked out of school. But I hadn't expected that, because you told me—"

"It's what I saw," Bruno said feebly. His mind flashed back to one of his conversations with Roberto. They'd been sitting in the park, enjoying another bright afternoon, when Bruno had expressed worries over his visions—how he might not be seeing all the good things he was sharing with people. But how he'd felt almost addicted to the rush of excitement upon giving even strangers good news.

Roberto had looked at him, nodded solemnly, and said to Bruno words he'd never forget. "If you believe it, Bruno, it's not a lie. Remember that."

"Then your power is a fraud," Antonia spat. She kicked dirt in Bruno's direction.

"You're a liar!" someone else yelled, but Bruno couldn't see who it was. The skies were too dark, and the crowd was too big. "You said I'd get the grocery job—and I didn't!"

The dam was broken. Bruno stepped back, overwhelmed by the harsh words and raised voices. He couldn't keep track of what people were saying. He just heard sharp snippets, threats, and most important—anger.

"... said my family would have a nice Sunday..."

"... get that jacket as a gift ..."

"... told me Benito did love me ..."

"... was actually right about Ivette's cooking..."

"... mi pobre perrito ..."

"... just another fraud ..."

". . . dunno, he was right that I'd win the contest ..."

"... gift is just some kind of parlor trick ..."

"... ashamed of yourself ..."

". . . would your family think . . ."

". . . hope you disappear . . ."

". . . dare show your face in Encanto . . ."

A long, low rumble of thunder cut through the complaints and yelling. Everyone looked up toward the sky in unison—the once subtle dusk now a menacing black. A shock of lightning cut through the sky. It felt like the entire town shuddered.

"M-maybe it's Pepa's doing—maybe she's in a bad mood or something," Bruno said. He knew before he spoke the words that they weren't true.

Roberto grabbed Bruno's arm. It wasn't gentle— Bruno could feel his friend's fingers digging into him.

"Don't listen to Agustín—or to any of them, Bruno, please," he said, the moonlight casting a strange shadow over his face as it cut through the trees. "You are doing what you need to do. But you've only just started. I'm here to help you, okay? I have been forever. I'm your friend. I want to be with you and in your family. You know that. I love your sister. Without you, it'll never happen, though. I'll always be on the outside—"

Bruno looked up at the sky again. Dark, monstrous clouds were converging somewhere nearby. He knew where.

Casita.

It was unlike any kind of storm Bruno had ever seen. Something was wrong.

"I—I have to go," Bruno said, stepping away from the group.

⊚⊚⊚⊚⊚

Bruno didn't remember anything else. Didn't remember turning around. Didn't remember pushing past Agustín, Roberto, and the crowd of villagers. Didn't remember running through the clearing and into the woods. Didn't remember screaming the entire way. By the time he snapped back to himself, he was on his knees, his arms and legs scraped and scratched by the branches, his breath coming in short, jagged bursts, and his hands covered in dirt. He'd been clawing. Clawing into the dirt. Trying to bury himself. Hide himself.

Trying to disappear completely.

PART III
THE FALL
OF BRUNO

Excerpt from Julieta Madrigal's Diary

I'm scared.

The skies are darkening.

Like a hand wrapping around the transparent globe protecting us all.

I don't need to be Bruno or Mami to know something is coming. Someone.

Bruno was right, in a way. Someone is going to betray us. But we won't know in time to move or react.

And that's the worst part.

Diary, I hope I'll write to you again.

But I'm not sure.

CHAPTER
THIRTY-THREE

Agustín Espinoza also ran, but in a different direction.

He ran toward La Casa Madrigal.

He had known the second Bruno slammed past him that he wouldn't be able to keep up with Alma Madrigal's only son. He also knew Bruno needed to be alone, needed to assess the damage he had caused—good intentions or not. And Agustín had been chilled by something else. The way Bruno's friend, Roberto, had looked at him—as if he was sizing Agustín up. Not as a friend.

But as a threat.

"Stay out of this."

Roberto had said those words a second before turning to chase Bruno. By the time Agustín had looked back, the mob of angry residents had dissipated and he had a clear path—toward help.

Agustín's heart ached for Bruno. He'd known of him as long as he'd pined for Julieta, and he'd always struck Agustín as kindhearted if a bit awkward. But Agustín was no bastion of normalcy himself. He was injury-prone and goofy and wore his heart on his sleeve. He had more in common with Bruno than he liked to admit. He saw a bit of himself in Bruno, and he felt a responsibility to help him—especially now, when he probably felt the most alone. It wasn't every day the entire town dressed you down publicly.

Agustín's breath caught in his throat as he approached La Casa Madrigal. In the cloudy moonlight, he had trouble making out what was going on—but he saw enough to know it wasn't good. A cloaked man stood in front of the house, looking up the front steps at Alma Madrigal, who seemed distressed. Things were escalating quickly, Agustín thought, and he had no idea what was really going on. He also knew he wasn't Alma's favorite person— just another suitor for her unmarried daughter, Julieta, and an unlikely one at that.

But it didn't matter—not now. He had to warn her that Bruno was in trouble. Whatever else was happening needed to wait.

He tried to stop his fast-moving feet but got caught in the dirt surrounding the front yard. Agustín muttered something as he pitched forward and slammed into the ground. He thought he let out a long moan as he lifted his head from the tough grass but wasn't sure. All he did know was that he'd interrupted whatever discussion was happening between Alma and the mystery man, and perhaps that was for the best.

The cloaked man turned around, and Agustín was finally able to place him—it was Francisco Padilla, who was around Agustín's grandfather's age. His attire was frumpy and messy, his unkempt beard decorating a gaunt, knowing face. He looked down at Agustín with a frustrated expression—one that said, *That was foolish*. Alma rushed down from the front steps toward Agustín.

"¿Agustín—pero qué pasó?" she said as she reached him, lending a hand to pull him back up to his feet.

He rubbed his head where he'd made contact with the ground. There'd be a bump tomorrow, he was sure, but overall he was in decent shape. He could worry about himself later.

"Perdón por la sorpresa, Doña Madrigal," Agustín said, genuinely embarrassed. "I had to rush over here—"

"Is it Bruno?" Alma's question struck Agustín as odd. Why would she immediately bring him up? Francisco stepped forward, as well.

"What is it, Agustín?" the older man asked impatiently. "Where is Bruno?"

"I mean no offense, Señor Padilla, but this is his mother's concern," Agustín said. His voice was kind but firm, and he thought he saw a flicker of admiration on Alma's face—which caught him by surprise.

Alma patted Padilla's arm gently. Not with affection, but with a camaraderie Agustín hadn't expected. Francisco Padilla seemed like a relic from another time. He lived outside the norms of the town but was always relatively pleasant when spoken to. Still, many avoided him for fear that he was tapped into some unknown, darker power they didn't understand. When Agustín had seen him here, standing in front of Alma, he had to admit his first thought was that Padilla was to blame. He still wasn't sure he was wrong.

"Don't worry, Agustín. Francisco came with a similar message," Alma said, shaking her head solemnly. "He's worried about Bruno, too. We were just trying to figure out what to do."

"About Bruno?" Agustín asked.

"In a way, yes," Padilla said. "While I have no gift—and don't wield magics of my own—I do sometimes get flashes of what's to come. And what I see is not good. For Bruno or Encanto."

"Well, that doesn't surprise me—especially after what I've seen," Agustín said, hastily running a hand through his disheveled hair. "I was talking to him—trying to help him figure things out—when we were surrounded. By neighbors. People from around town. They were all so . . . so angry."

"Angry at Bruno?" Alma asked with surprise.

"Yes, they felt he'd lied to them," Agustín continued. "That he'd given them false visions and they'd been wrong. They felt cheated."

Padilla gave Agustín a knowing frown, as if to say, *I saw this coming.*

"Where is he now?" Alma asked, her voice rising. "Where is Bruno?"

At the same time, Agustín looked at the main door of the house. Julieta and Pepa had appeared and were making their way down the front steps to the group.

"Agustín? ¿Qué haces aquí?" Julieta asked, her eyes on him. She wasn't upset. She seemed genuinely curious, which Agustín chalked up as a minor win. "Is everything okay?"

"Your friend came to warn us that Bruno was in trouble," Alma said over her shoulder, her tone kind and appreciative. "We're discussing what to do next."

"You said you felt a great imbalance in the magic of Encanto," Padilla said. "I feel the same—the future is impossible to predict perfectly, but I feel we are heading toward a very dark moment, Alma. This dangerous future is most certainly tied to your son. He means well, but he is lost. Someone has set him on this path, and we might be too late to stop him—or save the town."

"There's always hope," Agustín said. The others

looked at him with admiration. "I'll find Bruno. We can figure this out."

"Then we need to find Bruno now," Padilla said ominously. "There's no time left. The skies themselves are darkening. The mood of the town is growing more and more chaotic. There is a dangerous element in our midst, and Bruno Madrigal—for better or worse—may be our only hope."

CHAPTER
THIRTY-FOUR

"**W**e have to talk some sense into him," Pepa said, shrugging her shoulders in frustration. "He needs to cut it out with these fake predictions. Maybe that'll fix everything, no?"

Agustín noticed a small storm cloud forming above Pepa's head, sprinkling her with a light mist of rain. He didn't know her very well, but he didn't need to be her confidant to understand her mood was souring. She was not alone.

Alma seemed to be listening to Pepa, rubbing her chin as she paced around them.

"Yes, he needs to pull back, to stop with these lies," Alma said, disappointment seeping into her tone. "He, of all people, should know that the magic of Encanto is not something to be manipulated or toyed with. I've said as much to him. He needs to stop this immediately. We must—"

Agustín stepped in front of Alma and looked the Madrigal matriarch in the eye. He gave her a somber, kind look—hoping to connect with her as directly as possible. Because what he was going to say would surely upset her.

"It's not about what Bruno needs to stop doing, Señora," Agustín said.

"Oh, really?" Alma asked, her tone irritated. "Please explain to me how to manage my own son, Agustín."

"It's not about that, and I apologize if I've offended you," Agustín continued. He could see Julieta standing behind her mother, looking at him intently. "But Bruno needs to discover this on his own. He needs to figure out who he *is*, not who he wants to be, or who he thinks he has to be because of outside pressure. You're right—I don't know your son very well, but I do know what it's like to feel different. He needs time to figure himself out—and to find peace being himself. The longer he spends pretending or lying to others and himself, the harder this will be."

Alma waved him off and made her way toward the house. Agustín could tell she was frustrated. He tried not to take her actions—or her brisk dismissal—personally.

"Bruno understands the great responsibility we bear here," Alma said, sounding defeated. "We need to find him and talk some sense into him. The rest—that can come at its own pace. But for now, we need him to get his act together. To start thinking more about all of us and less about himself."

"That's what he is doing, Señora," Agustín said, his voice calm but focused. "If he did take a minute to care for himself, he'd see the toll this is taking on him. Instead, he's trying to make everyone happy."

Alma had continued into the house without stopping to listen to Agustín's response. He felt a hand on his arm. It was Julieta, looking somber but also . . . impressed?

"It takes a lot to talk to Mami like that," she said with a warm smile. "You held your own."

"I'm sure whatever tiny chance I had of winning your hand has been ground to a fine powder," Agustín said with a dry laugh.

"Oh, I wouldn't say that," she said, clutching his arm more tightly for a moment. "But we need to find Bruno now. To help him—one way or the other."

"I think he needs to hear that," Agustín said. "He needs to hear that you all support him."

"We love him," Pepa said. "He's our brother. We would never want him to be miserable—struggling to pretend to be someone he's not. I thought he was enjoying this act, that it was something he got a kick out of. But if not, then he should feel free to be true to himself. We love him no matter what."

"I don't doubt it, but he's been hearing the opposite from someone else," Agustín said, turning to Padilla, who gave him a subtle nod. "Someone close to him."

"Roberto?" Julieta asked. "He's Bruno's best friend. He cares for him. I see them together. They have a strong bond."

"Yes, Agustín, they're friends—do you know something we don't?" Pepa asked, sounding surprised and confused. "Has Roberto done something wrong?"

"No, not at all," Agustín said, raising his hands in mock self-defense. "I just know that Roberto has been supportive of Bruno. He could mean well. I know I've had many friends suggest I just—well, try to be different, to fit in better. But no one can question the influence Roberto has over Bruno—and if he's telling him to keep doing this, it's not helping. Not helping Bruno and not helping Encanto."

Padilla made a hoarse sound, like someone waking up from a long nightmare. Then they heard someone approaching. The entire group spun toward the figure walking up toward the house.

"What did I miss?"

CHAPTER
THIRTY-FIVE

The moment has arrived. The moment of action. For years, I've waited. Waited and watched as Encanto began to solidify itself. Not with me, not for me, but despite me. The Madrigals and their gifts lording over me like royalty. But I never wanted this. Never wanted to live in this supposed paradise.

But the cracks have been revealed. The fissures growing deeper—longer. As the skies blacken, as their gifts wane, as the candle flickers a bit too often—the time has come. Their only hope lies in a broken boy—Bruno Madrigal—who loathes himself so much he can no longer tap into the one gift that would have given me away. That would have shown them who was coming for them with time to prepare. No. He can't see me. Can't hear my footsteps coming. Wouldn't even dare imagine what's next.

I try not to savor the victory too much. But it'd be foolish to pretend I won't relish it. I can't help myself.

I've waited so long.

CHAPTER
THIRTY-SIX

Bruno's eyes fluttered open, and he saw nothing. A deep darkness. He blinked and shapes started to come into focus.

He was on the ground, looking up at the sky—which had become a menacing gray smear, the clouds covering any pocket of moonlight with looming, puffy shapes desperate to explode into rain. The wind was strong, pushing through the trees and foliage like an angry animal. Everything seemed to be shaking.

Bruno felt a dull ache and touched the base of his head. He winced sharply, the pain sudden and strong. This wasn't an injury from a fall, he thought as he slowly got up to a sitting position. Someone had hit him. But who? And why didn't he remember?

His last memory was of running—from Agustín,

273

Roberto, and the mob. Had they caught up with him? Had one of the townspeople reached Bruno and exacted angry vengeance for Bruno's mistake?

He'd never meant any harm, he thought. He wanted to help people. He wanted to do good. But had he gone too far?

Flashes of memory rushed back in bits and pieces, barely forming a larger picture. Rushing through bushes and branches, pieces of trees, and the forest scratching at his face. The sound of footsteps approaching from behind. His heart pulsing in fear, his breath becoming faster—short, desperate intakes—as he longed for more air, more time to get away.

Bruno rose to his feet. His knees ached, and by his touch, Bruno could tell they were badly scraped. His shirt was torn and stained. His new pants were ripped and ragged. His hair was out of place. All the things he'd done to change his appearance—to make himself someone else, to better connect with the people around him—were gone in mere moments. What was left? he wondered. Who was the person underneath?

The tears started to slide down his face, unbidden. He wasn't sobbing—his body wasn't shaking with sadness. He was too tired for that. He felt broken, dismissed, forgotten—standing here, alone on the edge of Encanto, wondering if anyone cared about him. The entire town considered him a fraud. His family saw him as an annoyance, a disturbance that had to be managed. But Bruno wasn't that. He wasn't an affliction or nuisance. He was a person, and he had feelings and trauma, too. He needed support, and it seemed like the only person in his life who even cared—

Roberto.

His face appeared in Bruno's memory, shrouded in darkness, behind Bruno, chasing him—a dark, dangerous look in his eyes. He was moving fast. Bruno could barely make out what was happening— but he knew it was him. Knew it was his friend's face chasing him through the trees.

A raised arm. A few words spoken that Bruno couldn't yet recall.

Had Roberto done this to him? No, it was impossible. Roberto was his friend. He'd been with him from the beginning. Supporting him. Cheering him on. He wanted to be part of the Madrigal family— not against it.

"Then why do I remember this?" Bruno said,

making his way back down the path he'd run through.

Was there no one out there to help him? Bruno thought. If Roberto had in fact betrayed him, was it because he'd been overcome by the mob's anger and fear of his own exclusion?

Was there an excuse?

He dropped to his knees again with grief, felt the sharp pain as his scraped skin made contact with the jagged rocks.

What was the point, then? Bruno thought. If there was no one to help him, no one to sympathize with him, why should he even bother?

A long, loud rumble of thunder.

This was not Pepa's doing. Bruno knew that. This was something else. Someone else.

He thought of surrender, of letting fate take over and sweep him away. Let the townspeople do what they wanted. Let his family ignore him. He would hide away, in his room, forever—alone and forgotten. Years from now, people would mention him in passing, like an imaginary person, a fairy tale, if they even dared speak his name. No one would talk about Bruno Madrigal, and that would be fine.

"No," Bruno muttered. "No . . ."

He stood up. He would not cave, or fold into himself. He would stop pretending to be someone he wasn't. He didn't want fake admiration or false love. He didn't want to appease strangers by being something he was not. He was who he was. Bruno was anxious. Bruno hated crowds. Bruno ate his food in a certain order. Bruno loved to read and lounge around. Bruno loved to imagine and pretend. Bruno liked hugs over handshakes. Bruno liked sitting on the grass and losing himself in the clouds and the trees. Bruno worried a lot. Bruno often thought about the worst possible scenario. But Bruno was also loyal. He loved his friends and family fiercely. He didn't know how to lie—at least not well. He didn't like to lie.

Well, most of the time, he told himself. He'd chosen a different path recently. Built on good intentions and kindness, but also on a foundation of falsehoods.

He had lied. He needed to come to terms with that, Bruno realized.

Sure, he was who he was, and that could not be changed—but he had to accept all the facets of himself. He didn't want to be someone else. He didn't want to pretend. Not anymore.

The mob had made him realize something. The truth was out now.

In that moment, with his mind empty and open, something strange and unexpected happened. He felt a familiar sensation, a buzzing around his eyes and head. He thought he saw that same thick green smoke in his mind's eye. And, as if it'd never gone away, a vision formed for him—clear and vibrant. Bruno felt like he was there. Felt like he could reach out and touch the people around him.

But what Bruno saw wasn't a pleasant peek into an idealized future. No, Bruno knew this was real. This was something barreling toward him—toward him and his family. And whatever frustration he had with his mother and siblings, this was a threat, something that could do incalculable harm to not only him but his entire world. If he didn't act, he wouldn't have the chance to be himself, to find out what he truly wanted out of his life.

Bruno had to save Encanto.

If he wasn't already too late.

CHAPTER
THIRTY-SEVEN

"**W**hy does everyone look so somber?"

Agustín, Julieta, Pepa, and Padilla seemed to each back up a half step as Roberto asked the question. Agustín noticed that he was smiling—that same calm, friendly smile. Agustín looked at Padilla, who was still wearing a stern look, except sharper—more worried.

"Where's Bruno, Roberto?"

It was Julieta. She stepped forward. She seemed relaxed, friendly. Roberto responded in kind, reaching out a hand for her, which she took briefly. After a few moments, she spoke again.

"Have you seen my brother?"

Roberto, still with that frozen smile, looked over at Agustín. A shiver ran through his body.

"He ran off," Roberto said, still looking at Agustín. *Is he challenging me?* Agustín wondered. "We were surrounded—there were a lot of people angry with him. You know how he is, Julieta."

He turned to face her again, taking her hand again and bringing it toward his chest.

"Your brother is feeling very isolated and alone," Roberto said somberly. "He feels very betrayed."

Julieta nodded. Agustín was confused. Why was she engaging with Roberto this way? Was Agustín truly worried, or was he jealous? He couldn't be sure. But he waited. He trusted Julieta. He would see what she had in store.

"I want to thank you, Roberto, truly," Julieta said. "For being such a good friend to my brother. He needed it. I'm just sorry we haven't been able to see him struggling."

Roberto's smile returned, sharper and brighter.

"It's the least I could do, Julieta," he said, stepping toward her. "You know how much I care for him, and for you. . . ."

His voice trailed off as his eyes scanned La Casa Madrigal—looking over the people who surrounded him. He lingered on Padilla, who could not hide his disdain for Roberto. Agustín swallowed hard as Roberto's face seemed to betray a flash of disdain at Padilla, as well. What was going on? he thought.

"I just want to be there for him, for you, for this entire family," Roberto continued. "I want to be a part of everything that is happening here in Encanto. To be close to you—your beauty, your light—would be my greatest privilege and thrill."

Agustín wanted to throw up. Was it possible to lay it on any thicker? he wondered. Esta locura was painful to watch, he thought. He saw something moving out of the corner of his eye. Padilla.

The older man stepped between Roberto and Julieta and placed a hand on Roberto's shoulder.

"Enough of this," Padilla said sternly. "Where is Bruno? You were the last to see him, no? Agustín said as much. Where did he go? Why isn't he with you, Roberto?"

"Remove your hand, old man," Roberto said, his smile gone, replaced by a sinister sneer. "You don't want to do that."

Padilla was undeterred.

"You've taken a strange interest in Bruno that doesn't feel genuine, Roberto, at least not to me," Padilla continued. "Why is that? What is it about our Bruno that you find so curious? And why are you so adamant he become something he is not?"

Roberto shrugged off Padilla's touch and backed up a few steps.

"You need to mind your own business, Padilla, for you are not without sin yourself," Roberto said, tilting his head slightly as if to say, *See, I can play this game, too.* "Before Bruno's gift appeared, you were the person people came to—the one who got all the attention. You'd play your cards, look to the skies—and maybe, if everything was aligned, you'd see what was to come. You were the person people visited to get clues to their future. Hints at what might be looming. Good news, hopefully, but sometimes not. How did it feel, then, when you were dethroned?"

Padilla shook his head incredulously.

"That's una basura," Padilla spat. "I've always cared for Bruno, like a son I never had. I tried my best to help him, teach him how to use his gift for the better. I have no jealousy—"

"You lie, Francisco Padilla," Roberto said, his tone calm and sly. "It's obvious to anyone here. Who benefits the most from Bruno being outed as a fraud? Certainly not me. I'm just his friend. I love his sister. I want to help him. But you—you suddenly become el jefe, the one who truly sees the future. Bruno is old news and you're the center of attention again. Did you think I wouldn't realize this?"

"That's not fair," Agustín said, stepping between Roberto and Padilla. "Francisco is a good man— we're all friends here. Why are we quarreling when we should be out there, looking for Bruno? Trying to prevent whatever this is?"

He motioned up to the skies, which were even darker now, with a tinge of red. A soft rain had started to fall, coating everything in mist.

"Get out of the way, Agustín. You're not some innocent," Roberto said. The kind, friendly Roberto was gone, Agustín could see. In his place was something more potent. Something darker. The true Roberto, Agustín thought. "You're not some unbiased arbiter. You want Julieta. You'd love for me to be out of the way. But the truth is, you can never have her. Why would she, a lovely, intelligent woman with a magical gift, spend any time with a clumsy oaf like you?"

The words lingered between them for what seemed like an eternity. Then Agustín watched as Julieta spoke.

"Roberto," she said. "You need to leave."

THIRTY-EIGHT

Agustín watched Roberto's face contort at Julieta's words. He was beyond upset. Padilla's accusation had seemed to push him over the edge. The veneer was not only cracking; it was being obliterated. Whatever was under the performance Roberto had been putting on was about to reveal itself.

Agustín felt someone next to him and saw Julieta by his side. She glanced at him.

"I want to apologize to you, Agustín," she said, regret tingeing her voice. "I thought Roberto was right—for a moment. I thought you were here, trying to help Bruno, because you wanted my attention. I thought Padilla had his own motives, too. But it turns out Bruno had more friends than I ever anticipated. And I feel bad about that. For not knowing what has been going on in his life."

Agustín sighed and smiled at Julieta.

"Bruno thinks he's alone," he said to Julieta. "He thinks no one appreciates him for who he is, so he needs to try to be someone else. Just to survive. Can you imagine how hard that is?"

Julieta nodded.

"I know what that's like," Agustín said. "I'm an awkward, clumsy guy—I wish I was a smooth talker, or better in conversation. Or more fun at parties. But I'm not. I worry. I sweat a lot. I am a messy eater. I have two left feet. But that's who I am. And I love myself. And Bruno needs support to get there, too."

"But we do love him," Julieta said, sounding slightly defensive. "He's one of us."

"When was the last time you told him?" Agustín said. Julieta raised an eyebrow in response. "Bruno wants to be loved for being himself. That's the only way he *can* be himself. He feels pushed away. Ignored. That's the sense I got from him. And the only reason I did was because I've felt that way myself so many times."

Julieta placed a hand on Agustín's arm, her eyes on him.

"You're a kind man, Agustín Espinoza," she said, smiling. "Bruno is not the only person lucky to have you in his life. I am, too."

"I'm not going anywhere."

Agustín and Julieta turned to see Roberto, standing in the same place, looking at them defiantly.

"Bruno is my friend," Roberto said, a low whine in his voice. "None of you have been there for him. None of you have tried to help him. Where were you when he felt alone? Where were you when he couldn't find a kind word? When he was desperate for love and approval?"

Julieta stepped forward.

"That's not fair to say, Roberto," she said. "We know now. We have always tried to be there for him."

"That's an easy thing to say," Roberto said, waving his arms. "It's easy to sit up here, in your ivory tower, and say you tried your best. Tan fácil. But the results are out there—you were ignoring what is happening in your own backyard, Julieta."

Agustín watched as Pepa stepped forward, and he

heard the crack of thunder above them. The rain got stronger, too. She was getting upset.

"You're scaring my sister," Pepa said. "And I don't think we want you here anymore."

"We need to find Bruno," Julieta said. "Please leave—or get out of our way."

The sound of shoes scraping on asphalt. A deep intake of breath. Agustín and everyone else wheeled around to see Alma, standing at the entrance to the house, her face stricken and scared.

"I know who it is," Alma said. "And I know why they are betraying us."

Agustín looked around at the gathered group. Roberto. Julieta. Pepa. He felt a sharp, sinking ache in the pit of his stomach.

Where was Francisco Padilla?

CHAPTER
THIRTY-NINE

Who will betray us all?

The thought hammered in Bruno's head as he ran toward Casita, his feet pounding the dirt, then the pavement. His vision—his gift—had returned to him. But not fully. He couldn't see it all. He couldn't see a face. But whatever he saw, it was not happening years from now, in a far-flung future. It was happening soon—in minutes. And he had to be there, to do something. To try to make a difference.

But was it Padilla, the mysterious cloaked figure who'd taught Bruno so much? Was it Agustín, desperate for his sister's love? Was it Roberto—a false friend with his own dark ulterior motives? Or, even worse, was it Bruno's own family—fed up with his actions and problems and eager to find a new path for Encanto, one not bogged down by Bruno's anxieties and insecurities?

Bruno stopped, sliding his fingers to either side of his forehead. He needed to know more. Needed to *see* more before he reached Casita. He needed some kind of advantage before he burst in trying to figure out what was happening. But was it too late?

Nothing came. Bruno felt that familiar flicker of energy—but it wasn't expanding into something more. His gift was still there, but it wasn't what it was before.

Had he done damage to the gift his mami and Encanto had bestowed on him? Was it too late?

"Bruno."

He opened his eyes. Francisco Padilla stood before him, hand outstretched.

"Qué bueno verte, mijo," the older man said, a soft smile on his face. "You've certainly looked better."

Bruno laughed. He gave himself a once-over. His clothes were smeared with dirt. He felt his hair—tangled and all over the place. It was a relief to see his old friend, even now, in what felt like the darkest hour for Bruno and Encanto.

"Francisco, you're here—what's going on?"

"I was hoping to ask you the same question," Padilla said.

Bruno gave the older man a hug, which appeared to surprise Padilla. "I-I'm just so happy to see you," Bruno said, his voice muffled. "I was looking for you, but then . . . What's happening?"

"Something is affecting Encanto," Padilla said. "Someone is interfering with you and your family— and I'm worried it might be too late."

Bruno stepped back.

"Are you all right? ¿Cómo te sientes?" Padilla asked Bruno, crouching down slightly to meet his eyes. "You're hurt?"

Bruno rubbed the back of his head and winced briefly. Someone—Roberto in particular—had hurt him.

"I made a mistake, Francisco," Bruno said sheepishly. "I tried to be something . . . someone else. I tried to use my gift to help, but it hurt people. They're upset with me. But I didn't mean for that to happen."

"Of course not, Bruno. Eres un niño bueno, sin mala intención," Padilla said. "But sometimes even our best efforts can have the wrong results. I'm sorry I couldn't help you sooner. To be there for you when you needed someone—even to just listen to you."

His friend's words lingered in Bruno's mind.

"I wish I could've been clearer in what I needed, what I still need," Bruno said, looking up at Padilla. "It's easy to suffer in silence, I think. To isolate and disappear. I hope I don't do that again."

Bruno stepped back.

"I just felt so alone," Bruno said. "It felt like I was the only one thinking these thoughts—that no one truly understood me. It feels so lonely. I couldn't understand what to do. I still don't understand."

Padilla nodded.

"Life is complicated, and we're all struggling to find clarity," he said. "There's no straight path, Bruno. We're all trying our best. All we can do is be thoughtful and transparent, and try to help one another find our own serenity. Your visions can provide only so much insight."

Bruno looked down at his feet, then back up at his friend. He felt a wave of relief, a wave of acceptance and understanding. Things that had been so hard to find for so long.

"What's happening, Francisco? Where is my family?"

"They are in trouble," the older man said softly. "They need you, Bruno."

"Then let's go," Bruno said. "Let's do some good."

CHAPTER
FORTY

"**M**ami, what is it?"

Agustín watched as Julieta ran toward her mother, Pepa a few paces behind. He couldn't shake Alma's expression—a potent mix of shock, dismay, and something else—something even more powerful.

Fear.

Alma Madrigal was afraid. Agustín had never seen this side of her, and he suspected that her daughters hadn't, either. What could scare her like this? What had happened?

And where was Francisco Padilla?

"Don't listen to her," Roberto said, his voice shaky. "She doesn't know what she's saying."

Agustín looked at him. Roberto's expression was cold, calculating. Like a predator sizing up its prey.

"What are you talking about?" Agustín asked.

Roberto pivoted to look at Agustín, his head moving slowly, as if following Agustín's every movement more on instinct than anything else. Then he smiled, finally recognizing what Agustín had said.

"Let me offer you some advice, Agustín," Roberto said, sounding different now—older, angrier. "Now's your chance to leave. To run. If you want to live, if you want to see another sunrise—you need to run, right now."

"I think you're the one who needs to leave, as I've already told you," Julieta said across the front yard, standing next to Alma, who was looking shaken and out of sorts. Pepa flanked her on the other side. "Whatever you are—you need to leave this village. You need to grant us peace."

Roberto let out a long, humorless laugh.

"Ay, Julieta—qué cómico. That's the thing, bella," Roberto said. "I don't have to do what you say. Not anymore. I don't have to live in the shadows. I don't have to pretend to love you or like your brother, or even enjoy being here, in this made-up town."

Agustín tried to step toward Roberto, but he moved fast—rushing past Agustín and slamming him to the ground. By the time Agustín had gotten to his feet, Roberto was across the way, standing inches from Julieta, a long curved blade in his hand—with the edge hovering just a centimeter from Julieta's neck. She looked like she was using every ounce of her strength to remain in control, to not scream in fear. Agustín wasn't sure how long it would last. He watched as Alma and Pepa backed away slowly.

"I know who you are now, Roberto," Alma said in disgust. "I know who you were. Why are you doing this?"

"Why, Alma?" Roberto responded. "If you have to ask, then you know absolutely nothing."

The blade moved even closer to Julieta's neck, and Agustín yelled.

CHAPTER

FORTY-ONE

It almost didn't feel real. Standing here. Fully revealed. In front of the accursed Madrigals, my blade in hand. The moment had arrived. It was happening. And there was nothing they could do to stop me. The game was over. I had won.

How long I'd struggled. How long I'd danced between the shadows, pretending to be something—someone—else. Forcing the smiles, dressing the part, making everyone around me believe I was Roberto, the joyous, happy, and carefree neighbor who did it all. Helped the elderly man across the street. Carried Señora Carvajal's groceries. Cleaned up the square after the annual festival. A good citizen. A kind man. A friend and confidant.

But I was someone else. A snake that had slithered into the pristine, magical land of Encanto with an agenda. A long game that was finally coming into play. A wrong long waiting to be righted.

I'd been an outcast. An orphan. A nothing, lost to my friends and family back home—a stranger. Only by sheer luck did I witness the lowest, darkest point the Madrigal family had ever experienced. The death of Alma's husband, Pedro. I felt sympathy for her—for them—then. But that vanished soon after. I trailed them. I witnessed the beginnings of Encanto. The house. Their gifts. I saw that even at their lowest point, this family stuck together. They supported each other. And they were granted gifts beyond measure.

Why do the Madrigals receive these gifts when I am the one affected by tragedy? When they murdered my father? Where was my gift? The world was unfair, and I wanted to fix it.

I knew what it was like to be poor. To struggle to survive on the streets of various small towns. Scraping and fighting for my life. I would be doing the same if I hadn't seen Pedro fall, if I hadn't had the wherewithal to follow Alma and her children to this new place. This new world.

And perhaps, if it had just been that—I would have truly wanted to be a part of the family. To have a real home, where I felt loved and embraced. A soft pillow to lay my head on. Warm, delicious food, siblings to play with. To know Julieta, Bruno, and Pepa. To be an ally and supporter. But the gifts came. And I saw the family become more than me. Greater than me. They were lording over Encanto like it was their private kingdom. Why couldn't I have a gift, too? What did I get from the loss I experienced? I was left with an aching need for revenge.

It was then, as I struggled to survive, that I knew I had to take it for my own. That I had to twist the magic that was spread out over the town and destroy it.

I had to bring about the downfall of Encanto.

And I finally saw with clarity. I discovered the way just a few short months ago, after years of searching. I found the key:

Bruno Madrigal.

CHAPTER

FORTY-TWO

Agustín's eyes darted between Roberto, clutching the blade to Julieta's neck, and Alma—standing just a few feet away, looking at Roberto with an anger and fear that Agustín could only imagine.

His mind was screaming. He had to act. But do what? he wondered. Agustín wasn't a fighter. That was more Julieta's territory. But he felt the pressure, could sense Pepa standing a few feet away, breathing heavily. The rain had intensified, a hard, pulsing downpour. That was most certainly Pepa's doing. But it wasn't enough. Something was distracting her from unleashing her full power, Agustín realized. How had this come to be? he wondered. How could one man with a blade stand inches away from defeating the Madrigal family?

And if that was possible, what could Agustín do to save them?

"Roberto . . . listen to reason, mijo, please," Alma pleaded. "Why are you doing this?"

Agustín, and everyone else, had heard Roberto's story—at least the bits and pieces he'd shared now that he had the upper hand. It sounded tragic, at least to Agustín's ears. A boy caught alone in the formation of Encanto, orphaned by the very magic that had blasted his father and the other renegade Colombian soldiers away, and then stranded in the small town, living on the edges of everything—trying desperately to fit in. He'd eventually found some semblance of a home with the Enríquez family, but that kind of trauma was hard to erase, even with the most caring and thoughtful role models. Still, why hadn't he reached out? Why had he let this resentment fester and boil inside him, until his only reason for being was to destroy the people who had built their home?

"Because it was the only way," Roberto said, his tone harsh and angry, in stark contrast to the smooth-voiced everyman he'd played before. The change was startling to Agustín. "Because you had it all and I had to struggle for any part of it. I'd been swept up in the magic of Encanto, trapped here by magic mountains without exit and fear of the unknown. I was alone."

He shook his head, looking away from Alma, losing track of the blade for the briefest moment. Julieta looked at Agustín. Their eyes locked for a second, and he understood what she wanted him to do.

"But why did you just hide for so long?" Agustín said, moving forward. His voice caught Roberto's attention, and he moved to face Agustín, eyes looking desperate and enraged. "Alma and her family would have helped you—would have tried to find you a home, a family."

"I didn't want a new family," Roberto spat. "I wanted the chance to find my own—to be free of this place, and of the people ruling it. I made it my life's goal to not only learn about the magic that kept Encanto going but to destroy it—so I could reap the vengeance I deserved! And I found a way to do it."

Agustín watched as Julieta sent an elbow into Roberto's midsection, distracting him momentarily and allowing her to wriggle free. She ran toward

Agustín as Roberto approached them, blade raised high.

"You were a good person, Roberto," Julieta yelled over Agustín at Roberto. "You still can be. Drop that knife. Listen to your heart. You don't want to hurt anyone."

The laugh that escaped Roberto's lips froze Agustín in place. A dark, shrill cackle—like a witch. The laugh of someone not looking for redemption, but revenge.

"But I do, Julieta," he said, taking another step toward them. "I need to hurt you, because it's my only chance—the only way I can get back to Colombia, back to my own home, and try to find my own family. I need to have my revenge on this town, and then the magical borders of Encanto will be shattered and will open, and I can finally leave and start a new life, on a blank page. As myself. Do you know what it's like to live your life pretending to be someone else? Always smiling, always cheering others on, always trying to be there for everyone else—when inside, you're broken? You're lost? When every new day is a reminder of the pain and isolation you hold inside? Do you have any idea what it's like to feel like every part of you is a fraud?"

"I do," someone said.

Everyone seemed to turn in unison to see Bruno, with Padilla a few steps behind, walking toward La Casa Madrigal. He looked calm and serene, hands raised in the universal sign of peace. He didn't want to fight. He wanted to talk. Agustín hoped Roberto would listen.

"Let us help you, Roberto," Bruno said. "Like you once tried to help me."

CHAPTER
FORTY-THREE

What Bruno saw seemed like something ripped out of his own nightmares. It was his darkest vision come to life—except now he knew who betrayed him. Who betrayed Encanto. And it broke his heart.

There stood Roberto, his best friend—the person he'd trusted with his deepest, darkest thoughts, who'd guided him through his greatest uncertainty—standing next to his family, waving a giant weapon at his sister Julieta and at Agustín. Alma and Pepa were nearby, looking on in abject fear. Had Bruno known? Had he ever considered the possibility that Roberto—sweet, patient, thoughtful Roberto—had been something else? That dark shadow following him and watching. An interloper trying to destroy their home from within.

At the same time, Bruno still felt sympathy for his friend, especially now—having heard his story from his friend many times, how he'd struggled to find a place after being uprooted, already an orphan. If only Roberto had spoken the whole truth, Bruno thought, this would have all turned out so differently. Bruno would have been able to extend a hand to him—to help him find his own place here in Encanto.

"You have to do something, Bruno."

It was Padilla, leaning close to Bruno's ear—the words like a giant, glowing sign in his brain. He had to do something. But what? How could Bruno stand up to someone like Roberto—strong, confident, fearless, unafraid of conflict? Bruno would rather hide under a rock than have an argument with anyone—much less intercede physically. But if he didn't, all Encanto would disappear—and everything his mother and his family had worked for would disappear with it. Was he willing to let that happen through his own inaction?

Padilla spoke again, this time with more urgency—a desperation and frustration Bruno had never heard from the older man.

"¿Bruno, qué te pasa? ¿No entiendes lo que

tienes?" he asked. "You can *see* what's next, my child. Do something—for you and your family."

Bruno tried to move. Tried to think about moving. Tried to plan anything that would get him out of this frozen state—but he couldn't. There was no vision coming. He would've sensed it by now. He was immovable, locked in by fear and panic, not to mention shame. Was this the legacy he was leaving in Encanto? That of a fraud and coward? Perhaps it was true, he thought.

"I can't, Francisco," he whispered. "I'm . . . I'm scared. I can't face Roberto. He's so much stronger than me. Confident."

"He is a fraud, Bruno," Padilla said, each word hissing out of his mouth. "He is a pretender who is trying to unravel the magic that holds this place together. Use your gift. Use it to your advantage. Before it's too late."

It is too late.

The words reverberated in Bruno's mind, and he started to vocalize them to his old friend and mentor—but before he could, Padilla ran forward, arms raised. He was aiming to take on Roberto himself.

Bruno stepped forward but immediately saw his path clouded by a familiar blurring—the onset of a vision. He saw Padilla engaging with Roberto, struggling to overpower him—only to be struck down violently and left on the ground, his life fading away like a faulty lantern. Before the vision could continue, Bruno screamed out. Padilla turned briefly.

"I saw it, too, mi niño bueno," he said with a somber smile. "But this was never my fight alone. Do your part, Bruno. Help save everyone."

And then Padilla turned around and ran toward Roberto, who spun to face the older man.

"What are you even thinking, viejo?" Roberto said, his face a sneer of defiance and anger. "Were you hoping to catch me off guard?"

Padilla pulled out a staff—perhaps it'd been a walking stick, though now the older man was wielding it like a weapon, with precision and confidence. Yet it wouldn't be enough. Bruno knew that much.

Bruno's breath shortened as Padilla stepped closer. At first Padilla held his own, but he was no match for the younger, more athletic Roberto.

"You've shamed this town, young man," Padilla said as he swung his staff down on Roberto.

It made contact with Roberto's blade, which almost cut the staff in half. Padilla stumbled back, pushed away by the force of Roberto's defense.

"Don't try to guilt me with your words, old man," Roberto said, now on the offensive, his blade raised high over his head. "If you're the last, best defense this town has, it's as good as mine."

"Your own actions shall be your undoing, Roberto," Padilla said, seemingly unfazed by his impending doom. "You've already lost."

As the blade came down, Bruno felt his mind and spirit leave his body—felt himself detach from what was going on, as if he were watching a play or dramatic reenactment of an old legend or fable. Anything to disconnect from the reality, the tragedy, that was coming.

Padilla screamed. Bruno watched Roberto's wild eyes take in what he'd done, then heard the soft thud of the older man's body hitting the ground. The rest of them gasped in unison.

Before anyone could speak, Bruno watched as Roberto lifted his head to face him—then everyone else.

"Is that all there is?" Roberto yelled, as if

performing a soliloquy for all to enjoy. "Are Encanto's meager defenses already spent?"

No one responded. Bruno let his eyes drift down to the crumpled mass that had once been his friend. He wondered what would happen next—and if he would be able to see it coming.

CHAPTER
FORTY–FOUR

Bruno had failed Encanto. He had failed his town. He had failed his family. He had certainly failed his friends—especially Francisco Padilla, who lay dead between him and his mother, sisters, and Agustín. Between them stood Roberto, his bloodied blade in his hand, his breaths short and ragged, his stare angry and fearless. What could he do? Bruno wondered. What chance did he stand against this kind of power?

Acting on instinct, Bruno bent down and gently removed Padilla's green cloak, then draped it over his own, smaller frame.

He watched as Roberto turned around and stomped back toward Julieta—his target. He saw Agustín, Pepa, and Alma tense up and brace for a fate like Padilla's. Bruno swallowed hard. His palms went slick with sweat. His body began to shake. His mouth was dry and the entire world seemed frozen in place, unable to move or continue until something else happened. Bruno had never been so scared—but he had to do something. Anything.

The vision was brief and fast—a jolt of sensory overload that almost sent Bruno toppling backward onto the grass. It was Julieta, in the grip of Roberto, the blade at her neck again—Roberto tossing around threats as he dragged Julieta back, back, back, and away from the family. It was happening in seconds, Bruno knew. It was happening now.

"Agustín, protect Julieta—he's coming for her!" Bruno yelled at the top of his lungs. He didn't care anymore, not about himself. He could bear dying— but not losing his sisters or Mami. His family. People who truly did care about him. Why had it taken this long to realize they cared? Why had he doubted them? There was no time to wonder that now, he thought. He hoped Agustín—this clumsy, kindhearted man after Julieta's heart—the only person who seemed to believe in him, would believe him now, would take a chance and prevent this dire future from rolling out.

He did. Bruno watched as Agustín stepped between Roberto and Julieta, and he felt a surge of respect and admiration for this man he barely knew.

"I can't let you do that, Roberto," Agustín said. It was clear he was nervous. His eyes looked panicked. But he didn't falter. Roberto was incensed. "I can't let you hurt Julieta."

"He won't hurt me," Julieta said, her eyes narrowed and angry. "He wouldn't dare. We Madrigals are tough to beat."

Thunder. Lightning. The rain grew stronger. Bruno watched as Pepa's expression continued to unfurl, the weather responding to her every whim. It felt like a monsoon was striking the town. But still, Roberto moved forward—blade raised and aimed at Agustín.

"You're not brave, Agustín—you're smitten. You're a fool," he said, every word a scream as he tried to be heard above the storm that pelted down on them. "You can't stop me. Pepa's rain cloud can't stop me."

Roberto swung the hilt of the blade at Agustín, knocking him back with ease. Bruno watched his friend tumble to the ground. Roberto hadn't used the blade itself, Bruno realized. He wondered if that meant his former friend was having second thoughts about what he was doing, or if he was as jarred by Padilla's death as everyone else. He wished he could ask him—just talk to Roberto and get him to listen to reason.

Julieta stood firm, arms raised in defense, but Roberto's blade stopped her from taking a swing. The storm started to dissipate. Roberto turned to Pepa, then to Alma, and finally to Bruno.

"You still have your gifts, your abilities," Roberto said, sounding louder and clearer now that the storm had been stifled. "You need to use them, if you want any chance to save yourself and this accursed town. You need to do whatever you can to let me out of this place. Or what happened to Francisco Padilla will seem like a pleasant daydream compared to what I plan to do to each of you."

He looked at Bruno, his anger seemingly sharper, more personal.

"Even as a failure, even as an impostor, Bruno— you let me down," Roberto said, shaking his head in dismay. "You couldn't even mess up right. I studied you, studied all of you, so much—and still, you failed. I knew that if you disconnected from your gift, if you perverted it into something else—there was a chance you could lose it. Or, even better—that the schism would create an opportunity to enact my plan, to defeat everything this town stands for. Instead, you couldn't even do that right. You had to hem and haw and almost ruin this for me—and for your entire family in turn. Now I'm just left with this sword, and this threat. But hear me now, Bruno Madrigal—if I don't get out of Encanto now, no one will survive."

CHAPTER
FORTY-FIVE

The irony was not lost on Bruno as he watched Roberto berate and scream at his family. The realization that, despite his best efforts—despite trying everything to mute and subjugate his gift—his visions had been true. He just hadn't expected it this way.

He had been betrayed. But not by Padilla. Not by his own family. By his dearest friend. And it was that friend, Roberto, who—as another vision had shown him—struck down someone he cared about. Now Francisco Padilla was dead, Encanto was on the brink of destruction, and Bruno still stood at a distance—feeling helpless and already defeated.

But there was a lesson in there, too, he thought—or was it another voice in his head? An older, familiar voice. Padilla's.

Listen to yourself, Bruno, and you will see not only what's to come—but what needs to be done, Padilla seemed to say now. Bruno tried not to think too hard about the source. Whether he was imagining his dead friend in his head or, by some twist of magic, Padilla was making a pit stop in Bruno's brain before disappearing into the afterlife. Bruno just tried to savor this last contact with Padilla, tried to hold on to this man who had meant so much to him. *Don't be afraid, Bruno. Be yourself.*

Bruno felt the presence of Padilla drift away, and he was left to watch the events before him continue to unfold. Pepa and Julieta huddled over Agustín, who was moaning and in pain, splayed out in the front yard, Roberto standing over them. Bruno saw Alma, his poor mami, talking to Julieta—outlining a plan. A possible path out. But it was not a feasible strategy. Not if they wanted to retain anything. Retain any hope.

"We could give him what perhaps he might really want—give him Encanto. Real power. Let him be in charge," Alma said, her voice shaking as Julieta looked at her, tears streaming down her face. "We have each other. We could leave Casita, safe and healthy. Find a new home. We need to protect our people—"

"No, Mami," Julieta said softly. "There would be no recovery from that. Everything we worked for—everything you discovered—would be lost forever."

Julieta is right, Bruno thought. That couldn't happen. He wouldn't allow it to happen.

The thought almost surprised him. The bravery. The directness. But it felt right. It felt natural. Despite everything he'd suffered, despite the darkness he'd witnessed, despite the fear and anxiety and isolation he'd endured just to survive—Bruno could not allow this to go on. Encanto wasn't just something his mami had made. Or something his sisters loved. It was his home, too. And he was a person, someone unique and special who deserved to be seen.

Seen for who he truly was.

His power had always been there. He just hadn't been listening to it. Bruno Madrigal realized in that moment who he was, and he loved that person.

He loved the Bruno who would care for a litter of stray cats found stranded near Casita.

He loved the Bruno who could make his sister

Julieta laugh so hard she'd be unable to catch her breath.

He loved the Bruno who brought his mami her cup of tilo at night when she seemed stressed.

He loved the Bruno who was a loyal friend and a good listener, the Bruno who liked sitting and watching people more than being the center of attention.

He loved the Bruno who was a helper, a caring brother, friend, and son—a good person. Flawed, sure—but kindhearted and loving all the same.

He couldn't be anyone else, even if he tried. He could grow—and he hoped he would over the years—but he also knew who he was inside, and he was tired of pretending to be something else. Of lying. Of hiding his true feelings. Of trying to gain favor by ignoring reality. He had a gift. It was high time he used it.

His mind flashed back—to long walks with Padilla, listening as his old friend shared sage advice. About life. Friendship. Loyalty. And family. He could smell the grass and hear the wind whipping past them. He felt Padilla's hand on his shoulder. He thought of the older man's coarse, liberated laugh. Padilla had just gone, but Bruno already missed him. He saw Agustín, basically a stranger to him, standing up to defend him—taking him aside and assuring him that the truth, the answer, rested in Bruno himself. That he only needed to look within to realize who he truly was—and who he should be. He remembered Agustín standing in front of him as the mob surrounded them, afraid but also brave— something to aspire to.

Then his mind shifted to something—someone— else. Roberto, goading him to dress differently, to talk boisterously, to ignore the gift that was so integral to his very being that Bruno had never even considered looking away. "Don't you want to be happy?" Roberto had asked. It had seemed so innocent then—so genuine and supportive. Finally, someone was paying attention to Bruno. But the attention had come at a price, and it was never about Bruno. Or for Bruno. He'd just missed it. Bruno had gotten it wrong. He'd believed his family didn't care for him—that they found him to be a nuisance. That he needed to be someone else to be loved instead of feared. That he had to bury the Bruno he was and replace him with something newer, shinier, and more palatable to the world. Roberto had egged him on. Bruno had felt apart from his sisters, apart from his mami—but Roberto had targeted them all. Roberto had banked on Bruno missing his plan.

Bruno stepped forward slowly, walking toward his mami and sisters. Roberto glanced at Bruno for a second, giving Bruno's approach a dry scoff.

"Seriously, Bruno, give it up," Roberto said with a shake of his head. "You screwed this all up. Let the adults handle this, okay?"

Roberto turned away and locked his eyes on Alma—as he waited for word on how she and her children would free him from the bondage of Encanto.

Julieta placed a hand on Bruno's and clutched it. They looked at each other.

"We will get through this," she said to him in a whisper—but a fearless one—her eyes on him, her other hand on Agustín's forehead. "We will be okay."

It had been so much more work, Bruno realized, to pretend to be someone else. The performance had been more draining than any of the sadness or solitude Bruno had suffered through in the years previous. By ignoring himself, ignoring his gift, Bruno had created a distance not only between himself and Encanto but between him and his own family. And as flawed as they all were—the gap made any kind of resolution impossible. Bruno saw this now.

He looked down at Agustín.

"How is he?"

"He's barely conscious," Julieta said. "Roberto must have hit him harder than we thought, because he's not doing well at all."

Bruno saw that his sister was crying now— a frustrated, angry cry. Julieta was many things, but helpless was not one of them. She liked to act. She wanted to help. In this instance, she could only sit and comfort this man she'd grown to admire in such a short time.

"It is my worst nightmare."

Bruno turned to see Alma, his mami, on her knees—holding her head. She looked shaken, completely unmoored. Bruno had never seen Alma like this. She'd always been the rock, the person he and his sisters and all the Encanto could depend on. But if even she was unstable, what hope did they have?

"Everything . . . everything we've worked for. The magic. Casita. Encanto," she said softly, almost to herself. "It's disappearing. And why? Because of a person I didn't know to help? How is that fair? Dios mío. What can I do?"

Bruno wasn't sure what made him decide to do it. Whether it was Agustín's pale complexion or Julieta's angry tears. Perhaps it was his mother's desperate words, or seeing Padilla die in front of him. But something propelled him forward, and before he could think about it any more, the vision had materialized in his mind's eye. It was not what he'd expected. But it felt right. And he was suddenly energized.

Just as the vision faded, he saw Roberto step closer, yanking Julieta away from Agustín and toward himself, the blade back at her neck. But Julieta wasn't having it. She sent the back of her head into Roberto's nose. Bruno heard a soft crunching sound, followed by a terrifying wail. Then Roberto was stepping backward—still clinging to his sword but no longer gripping Julieta, his free hand clutching his bloodied face, that strange wailing sound continuing like some kind of human alarm. Bruno stepped forward as Julieta backed away, rejoining Pepa and Alma near Agustín's prone form.

Something was happening. Bruno could feel it. He had seen what was next. But nothing was set in stone. He had to act on it. It wasn't about his visions. It wasn't about his gift. It was about himself—and how he could help his home, his family.

Roberto gathered himself, wiping blood away from his face, and looked up, wincing as if he were staring at the sun.

"What? Bruno?" Roberto said with a scoff as Bruno took a step toward him. "You're joking, right?"

Bruno didn't respond. He just took another step toward Roberto. The move seemed to have an impact on his former friend.

"Is this your way of scaring me, Bruno?" Roberto said, his voice slightly unsteady, like a child unsure if he was being pranked. "To walk toward me? I know you're a fraud—a joke. You were my puppet. What can you do to me?"

Another step. Bruno said nothing, Padilla's faded green ruana flapping in the wind.

"Seriously, ¿qué haces?" Roberto asked, his voice

rising in pitch—a mix of annoyance and fear. Bruno's silent act was working. But was it an act? "I could kill you with one blow."

Bruno stepped closer. He was a few feet from Roberto now. He wasn't shaking anymore. Bruno didn't feel fear. He wasn't angry, or on edge. He was at peace. He felt Padilla's words powering through him, could see the vision that had crossed his mind moments ago.

Bruno Madrigal knew what to do.

Not because of his powerful gift. Not because he felt pressure to see a certain way. Not because someone else said he should.

"Get away from me, you freak," Roberto growled—swinging the sword in Bruno's direction, the blade swishing just a few inches from Bruno's chest. But still, Bruno walked forward. Roberto took a step back. "Don't make me hurt you, Bruno. I don't want to hurt you if I can avoid it."

There it was, Bruno thought. Like hitting Agustín with the hilt of the sword. Roberto was hesitating. Feeling some kind of remorse and shame for his actions. Bruno took another step and stopped, his hands resting comfortably behind his back. He was not scared. He watched as Roberto's expression changed from concerned to terrified when Bruno spoke.

"Your future is calling you, Roberto."

CHAPTER
FORTY-SIX

He'd never tried this before. Had never imagined he could do it. Had honestly not thought it was possible. But Bruno Madrigal had no choice.

Bruno's gift—or at least the way he used it—had always felt like an intimate exchange. A peek into someone's singular future, a possible path they could walk alone. But here and now, as Roberto threatened not only Bruno's family but his entire life—he tried something else. He didn't just peek through the curtain to see what the future might hold for one person.

He did it for everyone. All at once.

And it shook Encanto to its core.

It started quietly as Bruno stepped forward—an eerie silence surrounding them all. Bruno would never forget Roberto's expression—a look that was

simmering with rage but also panicked and confused. The child overwhelmed by an adult reality.
Roberto was unsteady but still in control, and it was
up to Bruno to fix it. He'd thought long and hard
about what to do, how to offset what was going on,
and his place in it all.

Bruno had spent so much time in his own head,
letting his own demons guide him, that he'd lost
connection. To his family. To his home. To his real
friends. To the gift Encanto had given him. He'd
grown paranoid and afraid, and it had caused harm.

He knew in his heart that his feelings—of isolation, anxiety, otherness—were real. He wasn't
denying the truth—that he was an outcast. But he
had leaned into them so deeply—had made every
action and reaction part of a bigger narrative—that
Bruno had lost his place. He had become suscepti-
ble to influence. He wasn't sure about it before, had
only seen the visions that were easier to shrug off.
But now, with hindsight at his disposal, he recognized his mistakes.

First and foremost? Trusting Roberto.

The man who'd presented himself as his one true
friend—who had made efforts to separate Bruno

from his own family and allies like Padilla—was the opposite. An interloper with his own agenda, a plan so devious that it had not come to light until now. Roberto had manipulated Bruno, had taunted and teased and nudged until Bruno was convinced his entire family, entire community, was against him. He felt a great shame about that. But now Bruno also felt a great sense of clarity. He knew who he was, knew what he could do—

And he knew who he needed to do it to.

Roberto let out another confident, dry laugh. But Bruno could see a flicker of something else in his eyes. A slight hesitation. A recognition that things might not be going exactly the way he'd wanted.

"Your future is coming," Bruno said, his hands slowly rising as if he were trying to summon a great power from the ground. "Roberto, it's time we all see what's to pass."

Then it started. The green smokelike energy was gone, replaced by a bright light that seemed to start around Bruno's hands, then spread upward—creating a display not unlike fireworks. Green explosions of every size formed in the sky, some creating shapes. Loose ones at first, but then more detailed as the energy spread across the night air. The rain was gone, leaving a wide empty canvas—and Bruno's magical energies took full advantage.

The shapes and lights began to take clearer forms, creating a tapestry of images across the sky, large and visible to everyone. Bruno saw it all—as did Roberto, Julieta, Pepa, and Alma. It was a mirror of the town below, showing what was to come not just for one or two people but for everyone. It was in stark contrast to the darkness and dread Bruno knew the residents felt now, with their very being threatened. In its place was something else—hope. Bruno saw himself, still wearing Padilla's green cloak. He was looking out at the town, hidden. But Bruno realized something he hadn't noticed the first time this part of the vision had appeared to him. He was happy, in his own way. He was content. He saw Alma, older, wiser, surrounded by not only her children but an array of grandchildren—surrounded by love. Bruno focused briefly on a younger girl with glasses, her eyes heavy with resignation and insecurity. Bruno understood that, in time, he would know her—and help her, if he could. Bruno saw his sisters, Julieta and Pepa, with their husbands.

Bruno smiled as he noticed Julieta holding on to her partner, an older but still winsome and cheerful Agustín. Bruno glanced down and saw Roberto—his expression morphing from confident defiance to doubt. The vision was real. He knew that. He had known the power of Bruno's gift from the beginning. Bruno realized it, too. Roberto had messed with him so Bruno wouldn't be able to see Roberto's betrayal looming—wouldn't be able to use his gift to understand what was coming. And even then, under Roberto's spell, Bruno's gift kept trying to tell him something, that someone was going to betray him. But because of Roberto's manipulations, Bruno had doubted his own gift and his own family.

Bruno could feel it now—the powerful wave of love and energy residing not only in the vision of the future but in the present as everyone in the small town looked up and felt their hearts swell with hope and love. Bruno heard the murmurs, too. First confused, then excited, then evolving into cheers. The Encanto was abuzz with a joy and energy that Bruno had never seen. He watched as his sisters and Mami lit up with hope, with the certainty that things would be okay not only here and now—but in the future. Roberto was surrounded, everyone facing him. Bruno watched as more and more people from other parts of Encanto appeared in front of Casita—walking and looking up briefly to revisit the vision, like an epic painting on the roof, except it was a moving visual in the night sky. They all glanced at Roberto—nodding, shaking their heads, stepping toward him with movements that all said the same thing:

It's over.

Bruno watched as Roberto's defenses dropped. He stepped backward, off balance, as the communal vision dominated the night sky. It proved, clearly, that Roberto's future wasn't here and that his plan—however devious and powerful—would not work.

"It's done, Roberto," Bruno said, his tone calm and reassuring, not combative. He didn't want to hurt this person, this man he'd considered a close friend. But he did want to be clear. "You tried to break this town—to get between me and my family. But it's over. We don't want to hurt you, but we also don't want to be hurt."

Roberto looked around—at the crowd slowly stepping toward him, at the bright vision still playing out above them, like a dream come to life. Bruno held his breath. If Roberto was smart, which Bruno knew he was, he would surrender. He'd realize that there was no winning here. But Bruno noticed a hesitation. And he wasn't alone.

Out of the corner of his eye, Bruno saw Agustín move toward Roberto. He could tell that his friend had not recovered. His movements were clunky, desperate. Yet Agustín tackled Roberto. Bruno watched as they crashed to the ground and the wind was knocked out of both Roberto and Agustín. Julieta stepped back, watching the skirmish from behind, unnoticed by Roberto. Roberto rolled Agustín off him with ease. In a moment, he was standing over Agustín, arms raised and ready to strike.

Bruno moved between them. His eyes met Roberto's.

"Step aside, Bruno," Roberto said, his expression a jagged scowl. "You don't have the mettle for this. You think you've won because of your little fireworks display? You haven't. I'm not broken or defeated. I still have options. And your little friend here—he can't stop me, either. So let me finish him, and then let me out of this accursed town."

Bruno had never been a fighter. He hated confrontations of any kind. The idea of facing off against anyone, even verbally, sent shivers through his entire body. But he was also a loyal friend, and a defender of his own.

"I will protect my friend," Bruno said, positioning himself more solidly between Agustín and Roberto. He could hear Agustín moaning, the exertion taking too much out of him in his fragile state. "That's what I do. Agustín was there for me when I needed him. You weren't. You took advantage of me, Roberto. Tried to trick me. Manipulated my gift and my life so you could get away. But I am who I am, and the real Bruno—the person I am inside," Bruno said, tapping his heart, "is a true friend. Not the person you wanted me to become. A pretender. Someone who lies and connives. Someone who hides who they are to be liked. I'm myself again, Roberto, and no one—not you, not Encanto, not anyone—is going to change that."

Roberto rolled his eyes and stepped forward. He raised his arm, his mouth open, ready to share a sharp retort. But the comment never came. Bruno heard a soft thud and watched Roberto crumple to the ground. Standing behind him was Julieta, a knowing smirk on her face and a large plank of wood in her hands. Pepa and Alma rushed to her side and embraced her as they all looked down at the unconscious Roberto.

"He shouldn't have gotten so cocky," Julieta said. "He underestimated us."

"Never underestimate the power of family," Alma said, wrapping one arm around Julieta and the other around Pepa. "Never underestimate the power of love."

Bruno stepped back and watched as a few townspeople gingerly lifted and carried the unconscious Roberto away. They walked him toward the town doctor, with the same care they'd give to a newborn, regardless of Roberto's efforts to destroy their very way of life. Bruno's heart warmed over. He looked up. His vision—the one that united everyone's futures—had started to fade, replaced by the dark of night. Bruno took a long breath. The hustle and bustle of the town slowly inched back to normal. He watched as Julieta helped Agustín to his feet. Saw Alma and Pepa start to pick up the debris from the skirmish. Heard the gossip and conversation of

Encanto returning. The electric anxiety and excitement were gone, replaced by the soft murmur of what was before.

Bruno should have felt a wave of relief. They'd survived. Roberto was defeated. Encanto lived on. His family was safe.

But Padilla was dead.

And why couldn't he shake the feeling that everything had been his fault?

CHAPTER
FORTY-SEVEN

I lost. Lost it all. Defeated by my shortcut. The person I thought would be last in line to stop me.

But Bruno surprised me. Surprised us all. He showed strength and determination when I'd written him off.

Now I sit here, in this tiny room, alone—watching the accursed village through my tiny window—and waiting.

Waiting for my sentence. Waiting for my fate. What do these Madrigals have in store for me? If they can't set me free—what do they expect me to do?

The mother, Alma, comes by my room daily. To chat. To watch me eat. She's patient. Kind. Part of me wants to let go. To talk to her and open myself up. But the rest of me doesn't. The rest of me wants to keep my defenses up forever. To string it out until they have no choice but to do their worst.

But perhaps there's another way. A softer path.

I'm not sure yet.

I see Bruno walk by from time to time. He doesn't know I'm in here. That I can see him.

He was the wild card. The one who surprised us all.

The real Bruno Madrigal is not to be trifled with.

I learned that the hard way.

CHAPTER
FORTY-EIGHT

"You have to talk to him," Julieta declared as she handed the old broom to Agustín.

They were standing on the front porch of Casita, tidying up. Pepa and Félix had wandered off to the center of town, and Agustín had lingered to spend time with Julieta. He'd been excited. He hadn't expected a lecture about her brother, though.

"About what?" he asked, sweeping leaves and dirt from the front steps. "Your brother just needs to be by himself, Julieta."

Agustín slipped on the porch and felt his bottom slam into the stone. He winced. Julieta came up behind him and helped him to his feet.

"¿Agustín, pero no tienes ojos?" Julieta asked with a laugh. "There's a giant crack in the steps. You must watch what you're doing."

Agustín laughed.

"I guess I just want more of that food of yours," he said with a smile. "It always makes me feel better."

Julieta smiled back.

"That's the idea," she said.

A silence lingered between them, not the uncomfortable kind but a pleasant, warm one. Like she knew something he had missed. They'd spent most of their free time together since the incident with Roberto, as if spurred to make the most of their days in the wake of such a surprising turn of events. What Agustín had long ago written off as impossible was starting to seem like something that could happen. Or could it? he wondered. Could Julieta ever consider . . . *him*?

Julieta took Agustín's hand.

"My brother looks up to you, Agustín," she said, holding his hand tightly. "I want him to know that we all support him. That we love him. We can't risk what happened here happening again."

She motioned to the front lawn, recalling the battle with Roberto.

"Please tell me you'll help," Julieta said, her voice pleading.

"Your brother is stubborn and independent—we can't just stand here talking about him and expect anything to happen," Agustín said. "But he does care for you—and for Encanto. I think reminding him that everyone cares for him, too, will help."

Julieta nodded in agreement.

"Great, so it's settled," she said. "You'll talk to Bruno. When you return, you'll have a bite of the caldo I'm making and feel instantly better."

"What more could I want?" Agustín said.

He leaned in and kissed Julieta. They both seemed surprised after it happened. But neither seemed unhappy.

The words felt true to Agustín, especially now.

What more could he want than this?

CHAPTER
FORTY-NINE

He could have prevented it all.

This was all my fault.

The thought stuck with Bruno long after the night's chaos was resolved. The wreckage hastily fixed. Agustín's injuries healed. Roberto given time to think about what had happened. His mami, Alma, didn't normally have vengeance in her heart, but she'd never seen someone get so close to destroying everything she cared for. She wanted not only to understand what Roberto had done but to determine a fair punishment. She spent hours talking with Roberto each day. The first few days were nonstarters—with Roberto refusing to engage. After a while, they spoke—brief, halting conversations that went awry faster than they started. By the end of the first week, they were sharing meals together.

It was before one of these trips that Bruno intercepted his mother. His stomach was twisted. His palms were sweating. But he knew he had to speak to her. There was something he needed to discuss with her, and it couldn't wait. Even now, after so much pain and heartache.

"Mami, do you have a minute?" Bruno asked, picking up his pace to match his mami's swift stride.

"Bruno, I was about to visit Roberto for one of our chats," she said, looking harried. "What is it?"

Bruno swallowed hard.

"Mami, this is hard for me to s-say," Bruno stammered. "But I'm trying to listen to my gift more. To not change it or twist it."

Alma froze in her tracks, her expression concerned.

"What is it?" Alma asked. "Did you have a vision?"

Bruno nodded.

Alma stepped closer to him.

"What was it, Bruno?" she asked, placing her hands on his, meeting his eyes. "Are we in danger?"

Bruno shook his head quickly.

"No, Mami, no—I don't . . . well, I don't think so," Bruno said, looking at their hands clutched together, like forged metal—a chain. Twisted and bent but unbreakable. "But I do think we need to be ready."

"Ready for what?"

"In my vision, Mami, la velita—the candle— it was flickering," Bruno said. "And the power of Encanto was fading. There was darkness, and light— and someone standing in front of it all. I couldn't make out who, though. We were all in trouble. It wasn't tomorrow. It was some time from now. But I saw it. Everyone was worried."

Alma's expression softened a bit, as if the sug- gestion that the vision was years from now made it less dire.

"I just wanted to tell you, Mami, so you could be ready—so you could stop it from happening," Bruno said. "Don't be hesitant like me. Don't avoid it."

Alma let out a long sigh.

"Where are you in this vision, mi hijo?"

"I—I don't know, Mami," Bruno said. "I didn't . . . I didn't see myself."

He tried to be mindful of what he said, because it was true—Bruno didn't know where he was. He could only go by what he'd seen in the vision. But it affected his mother regardless. He watched as her shoulders sagged. A moment later, though, she straightened up and pulled him in for a tight hug.

"We will figure it out, Bruno," she said, her cheek on his. "I know we will. Thank you for telling me this."

"Are you scared, Mami?" Bruno asked.

Alma seemed surprised by the question but considered it nonetheless.

"I am . . . wary, Bruno, that is all," she said, choosing her words with care. "I believe your visions. I believe you. But I have dealt with prophecies and predictions for my entire life. It's why I doubt people like Padilla, even though that was a mistake. I worry that too much of our lives feels written already, and we're just going through the motions. But that's not life, mijo. There's so much to be done. To be enjoyed. I don't want any of us to feel tied down to something that might change at the drop of a hat. Does that make sense?"

Bruno nodded. Alma pulled him into another

tight hug, kissing the top of his head like she had when he was much smaller.

"I love you, Bruno," she said. "Con todo mi alma."

Bruno smiled at the joke, of Mami using her own name to express her love for him. It brought a feeling of warmth over him.

"I have to go," Alma said hesitantly.

She stepped back and spun around, waving to Bruno as she made her way to meet with Roberto, made her way toward building a difficult and genuine peace with the man who almost destroyed Encanto. It would not be an easy task.

Alma's goal was simple: make Roberto understand that he had to accept responsibility for his actions. Convince him that there was a life after that punishment, too. That even now, under the weight of all he'd done, Roberto could still help the village continue to build something special. Roberto seemed to feel some shame for his actions and wasn't keen on being locked away forever. But Alma had another plan for Roberto, and how he might make amends.

"We are not a prison, Bruno," Alma had told her son after one of her long sessions with Roberto. "We didn't build this place to hold our residents in an airtight grip. But he did wrong, very wrong. He is a murderer. He will have to spend many days alone, as an outcast, until he is deemed ready to return—until he has come to terms with what he's done and is ready to make amends to those he has harmed. Even then, I told him, I cannot promise he will be welcomed with open arms."

Bruno let his mother's words linger in his mind. An outcast, Bruno thought. Padilla appeared in his thoughts suddenly, and he couldn't avoid realizing the connection there. He started to ask his mother, but she was already a few yards away.

"What did you want her to do, Bruno?" Pepa had asked him later, when he approached his sisters with the news. "Mami isn't a dictator, niño. She's earned her place through respect and trust. She spent a lot of time figuring this out. Roberto will have to come to terms with what he did—and then we'll take it from there."

Julieta nodded as she prepared some pandebono for the evening's meal.

"It's fair—and more than he deserves, I think,"

Julieta said. "He killed Padilla, and he hurt Agustín—for starters. He should be thanking everyone he sees for Mami's kindness."

"But isn't this what Roberto wanted?" Bruno asked. "To get away from us all?"

The sisters turned to him and scoffed in unison.

"Reality comes at you fast," Pepa said. "Roberto had plans for us, to make us pay for what happened to him as a kid. But do you think he really thought it through? Did he really consider what he wanted?"

Bruno's nose scrunched up.

"I guess you're right," Bruno said, shaking his head slightly. "I hope he learns about himself while he's alone. I hope he realizes no one wanted to hurt him."

"Only time will tell, hermanito," Julieta said, placing an arm on his shoulders and giving him a placid, loving smile. "All we can do is show kindness and forgiveness to people, even the ones who want to do us harm. Roberto is smart. I hope he accepts it, too."

⊚⊚⊚⊚⊚

The last time he saw Roberto, it was a few weeks later. He was dressed in simple clothes—the kind of light outfit you wore when you were going on a long hike. He also wore a large hat and bulky backpack. Alma was with him, and they were walking away from the town square. Bruno called out to them when he caught sight of the duo.

"Bruno, don't worry, I will be back," Alma said.

"Roberto—where are you going?" Bruno asked.

Roberto motioned toward the far side of the village.

"You won't see me, Bruno, don't worry. Your mami set up a place for me on the far edge of Encanto," he said, looking at his feet. "I will be there for a while. I won't want for anything—except other people. But it's what I need to do. I appreciate her kindness—especially after . . . well, everything."

"Well, what did you expect, niño?" she said with a dry laugh. "That we'd leave you to rot in a cell?"

Roberto flinched. It was exactly what he'd expected, apparently.

"I'm glad you'll be able to think, Roberto. I hope you understand no one wanted to hurt you. I really considered you a friend," Bruno said, slapping him on the shoulder. "I hope in the future, we can be friends for real. Without deception."

Roberto seemed touched by the statement and gave Bruno a quick, awkward hug.

"I'm sorry for what I did to you, Bruno," Roberto said sheepishly. "I am sorry I hurt you to get what I wanted. If only I'd—if only I had asked your mami, or tried to be more direct, we could have avoided it all."

This was all my fault.

The words screamed inside Bruno's head, but he pushed them aside.

"We all make mistakes," Bruno said with a nod before stepping back. He waved as Roberto started to walk away from the town square. He expected his mami to follow, but instead she hovered near Bruno, expectantly.

"He will be fine, Bruno," she said softly. "We all will."

Bruno blurted out his response.

"But will I be fine, Mami?"

Alma's eyes widened.

"¿Qué dices, Bruno?"

His throat tightened. His body tensed up. He

didn't want to talk about this. Not with his mami, not with anyone. But the weight was starting to wear on him, and if he'd learned anything at all, it was that keeping these thoughts in could hurt more than help. So he let them out.

"I could have prevented all this, Mami. If I'd listened to you, to Padilla, to myself," Bruno said, his despair simmering with each word. "I wouldn't have been so distracted. I wouldn't have been so easily manipulated. Into following Roberto. Into giving those false visions. I was just trying to help— to make Encanto safe and happy for everyone. What really helped was showing people the truth—that the future was bright, for all of us. But if I hadn't been tempted to ignore my own—my own gift . . . It put everything at risk."

Alma placed a hand on Bruno's face, the warmth of her fingers like a powerful jolt.

"Bruno, we are always here for you, no matter what," Alma said. "We are here to help you with this journey, just as you are here to help us. ¿Entiendes?"

Bruno nodded. Alma pulled him in for a hug, then stepped back to look at him.

"I'll be back, mijo," she said. "We can talk more,

okay? Don't be so hard on yourself. We all make mistakes."

Bruno smiled wanly as he watched Alma and Roberto walk away. He might never see Roberto again. He felt a pang of sadness for the friend he'd imagined, the real friend who could have been. Perhaps in another time, he thought. Or in a future he couldn't see yet.

Bruno wandered the edges of Encanto alone for what seemed like hours—kicking rocks, stepping in puddles, watching the town bustle along from a distance. He felt like he could do this forever—live on the fringes of Encanto and not participate. Hadn't he abdicated that role? he thought. Didn't his mistakes come with a sentence, too? Should he even remain in town, or be punished the same way Roberto had been? He wasn't sure. He didn't want to explore that too much.

"You look pretty down for a hero," someone said.

Bruno turned around to find Agustín, smiling broadly, standing a few paces behind him.

"Hero? You must have me confused with someone else," Bruno said.

Agustín caught up with him.

"Your sister said I'd find you here," he said. "'He's sulking and needs a friend,' she told me. Is she right?"

"Julieta is always right," Bruno said with a laugh. "I'm glad you two are spending so much time together."

"Your sister is very special," Agustín said, his tone suddenly serious and introspective. "But that's not why I came here. You ignored my question: What's the hero of Encanto doing lumbering around like some kind of pariah? You saved us all."

"It's my fault we were even in that position, Agustín—but thank you for the kindness. If I hadn't ignored my gift, or fallen prey to Roberto's machinations, none of this would have happened," Bruno said, starting to walk down a worn path, shaking his head. "If I'd been smart enough to see through his facade, I never would have been tempted to ignore what my visions told me."

"What did your visions tell you?"

"That . . . my f-future . . ." Bruno stammered. "My future was dark. I was alone. Scared. Isolated. I was living in the house, but apart from everyone.

I was unhappy. I was a stranger to my own family and town."

"So you pretended you were someone else, to . . . what? Stop that?" Agustín asked.

"Yes, I thought that if I tried to be someone else, I could prevent that vision from happening," Bruno continued. "But that's what Roberto wanted. He wanted me distracted so I wouldn't see what he was doing. He was the one who betrayed Encanto. And it's my fault."

Agustín placed a hand on Bruno's shoulder.

"Bruno, you can't beat yourself up over this," Agustín said. "It will only hurt you. No matter what happened before, you saved us all."

"I didn't save Francisco," Bruno said sharply. "Francisco Padilla is dead."

Agustín nodded solemnly.

"That's true," he said. "But your gift came through at the right time. And everyone is grateful to you. You kept the magic going. When it mattered, you listened to your gift. And it delivered."

Bruno tried to speak, but the words got stuck in his throat. Agustín seemed to notice it, too.

"I'll leave you to your thoughts, Bruno," Agustín said, patting Bruno's arm gently before he stepped back toward the town square. "But I wanted you to know how I feel. How we all feel."

Bruno started to respond, but Agustín interrupted.

"And one more thing," he said. "That vision? The one that scared you?"

Bruno nodded.

"The one that made you think you had to change everything about yourself?" Agustín said. "What if it was wrong, Bruno? What if—I dunno—the magic was so messed up, you didn't see it right? Did you ever consider that?"

Agustín smiled, then turned around, leaving without another word. His question seemed to float between them as he got farther away.

Did you ever consider that?

He walked toward a small rock—just large enough to sit on. Bruno rested on the rock for a moment, watching Agustín disappear into the distance, listening to the sounds of Encanto.

He'd lost so much, Bruno mused. His friend Francisco Padilla. The trust of his neighbors. Himself. But nothing was irretrievable, he realized. He had tried so hard to ignore himself—to ignore the person he knew he was—that he'd become someone else. A false Bruno. What a terrible, painful cell that would have been, he thought. Spending the rest of his life pretending to be someone else, just to avoid a fate he wasn't yet sure was happening. In his desperation to not become that person, he'd become someone completely different—but no closer to the real Bruno.

He waved a hand in front of his face and took a deep breath. He wasn't sure what he would see. But he needed to know. He needed to be sure.

The vision formed fast, and it lasted for a moment—but Bruno saw enough. It was him. Older, wearing Padilla's tattered ruana—looking more beat-up than it was now. He was in a dark, mysterious place. But this was different. This was not like the vision from before. Yes, Bruno was alone—yes, he was hiding somewhere. But Bruno could sense something different, something almost joyous. He looked closer and could see his own face.

Bruno was smiling.

As quickly as it had appeared, the vision fizzled.

Was it the same vision as before? Bruno wondered.

Had he done enough to avoid what he'd feared—merely by being himself instead of pretending to be someone he wasn't?

Bruno sighed.

There was no way of knowing. Even seeing this—a vision of an older Bruno, smiling and seemingly happy—Bruno knew that nothing was carved in stone. Still, it gave him hope—hope that he could navigate the choppy waters that lay ahead. Bruno had work to do, with his family, with his community, and—most important—with himself.

The real Bruno. The person he was inside.

Never again would Bruno try to be someone else. Never again would he misrepresent his gift to appease others. He couldn't pretend to be what he *thought* others—like his family or his neighbors—wanted him to be. He was Bruno Madrigal. An outsider. An introvert. Anxious. Shy. But also a loyal friend. A good brother and son. A believer in the magic of Encanto. A hero.

And most of all?

Bruno Madrigal was one of a kind.

CHAPTER
FIFTY

Twenty-two years later

Bruno watched as the door disappeared, like dust falling to the floor. He couldn't see her face, but he saw five-year-old Mirabel's head bow. His heart seemed to stop as the candle, held gingerly by his mami, flickered ominously. The gasp from the crowd seemed to be universal. Everyone was surprised. No one had considered this—that one of the Madrigal children might *not* receive a magical gift.

And no one knew what it meant.

Bruno took a step back and watched as everyone seemed to focus on Alma Madrigal—with their questioning eyes, their desperate frowns. Bruno waited as the crowd remained on the ground floor below the wide, curving staircase. Then he moved slowly and carefully up the steps. He placed a hand on his niece's tiny sagging shoulder.

"It will be okay, Mirabel," he said softly.

His niece, her tiny body shaking softly, turned to him. He saw the tears welling up in her eyes. He wanted badly to tell her it was a joke, that everything would be fine. But not this time. Something had gone wrong, and even Bruno couldn't figure it out.

She didn't give him much time to think. Instead, she leaned into him, giving her uncle Bruno a strong, tight hug. A piece of Bruno seemed to turn to dust, too, with each choking sob he heard as his niece cried.

6\96\96\9

Alma Madrigal's shadow appeared in the hallway as Bruno made his way down. He noticed it immediately. He'd been expecting her.

A few hours had passed since the ceremony, since Mirabel hadn't received her gift. The people had cleared out. Mirabel was asleep. Bruno knew this only because he couldn't hear her sobbing or his sister Julieta's soothing voice, trying to calm

CHAPTER FIFTY

her daughter. Bruno had known Alma was coming here because he couldn't hear her pacing anymore, her worry enveloping all of Casita—and all of the Encanto. Something was very wrong with the magic. You didn't need Bruno's gift to see that.

"Bruno," Alma said, her voice a pained croak. He could barely make out her features in the darkened hallway. "Tenemos que hablar."

Bruno stood up and met his mami in the doorway.

"What is there to talk about, Mami?"

There was a moment of silence, and then Alma Madrigal stepped into the room.

The moonlight peeking through Bruno's window shed light on how much Alma had changed in just a few hours. Gone were the energetic smile, the wide eyes, the eager expression—all parts of every gift ceremony, as many as Bruno could remember. In their place was a gaunt sadness—a look of utter defeat that Bruno had never seen on his mami's face before. It broke his heart.

"We are in grave danger, Bruno," Alma said, her voice quivering. "Never before has a gift not arrived. I've never seen the candle flicker like that. I must know what is coming. I need your help."

It clicked in Bruno's mind then, why his mami was here. Not to be consoled. Not to see if Bruno was okay. But to ensure that Encanto remained strong—to ensure that the magic that had brought them all here was not at risk of disappearing. It was pragmatic and practical, but it was also not what Bruno wanted. In times like these—in moments of darkness—Bruno wanted to feel comfort. Security. Not strategy. He loved his mami, but he also understood her flaws. She'd spent the majority of her adult life trying to keep Encanto going, keep the magic alive. What had happened earlier that night was a jarring blow, and she was reacting rashly.

He'd also warned her about this.

He thought back, to years before. To Roberto's defeat and the vision Bruno had seen. Of a looming darkness and threat to the village—a light flickering sharply. His mother had shrugged him off, had acted like it didn't matter. But here it was, Bruno thought. And they were not ready. He let out a long sigh.

"I don't know if I can do this, Mami," Bruno said softly, shaking his head. The truth was, he didn't know if he *wanted* to do this. Magic acted in strange ways. Bruno was wary of trying to stay a step or two ahead of Encanto's. "Mirabel is the one who needs our help now. Our love and support. She's hurting."

Alma's mouth tightened.

"Mirabel will be fine," she said. "If we preserve the magic of Encanto. Otherwise, we will all be back where we were years ago—wandering the jungles and countryside, desperate to find a home amidst the darkness. Is that what you want, Bruno?"

The blade of guilt poked at him hard, a weapon only his mother could wield with such precision. On one hand, she was right. But that didn't mean it was the only path.

"I want everyone to be happy," Bruno said, meeting his mami's eyes. "The rest is secondary."

Alma placed a hand on Bruno's chest and met his stare with desperate, pleading eyes.

"Bruno, por Dios, listen to me—look into the future. Find out what is happening to Encanto. Please. We need to know. We need to prepare," she said. Her chin shook slightly. "I would not ask this of you if I had any other choice, mijo. I need to know."

Bruno swallowed hard.

"And will I be judged for what I see? Will I be

the bad guy if it isn't good?" Bruno asked. "I can't control what my visions show me."

Alma patted Bruno gently and turned toward the doorway.

"I understand, Bruno, of course," she said. "But please know—if what you see is darkness, then we will have much more to worry about than whether you are at fault or not."

"So it's up to me, Mami?"

Alma's eyes narrowed slightly.

"We all need your vision to help us, Bruno," she said, her voice stronger now—as if buoyed by some unknown force. "Do not let me—your entire family—down."

She stopped at the doorway and looked at him again, her eyes heavy and distant. Bruno didn't realize then that it would be the last time he'd see her for a decade.

A few hours later, the vision came. It was like the one he had seen all those years before—the one he'd warned Mami about. But different.

Because now Bruno could see what was at the center of it all.

He could see Casita, looking as it did on any given

day, the skies bright, people milling around—a sense of peace and joy in the air. A second later, it was dark outside, a storm swirling around the house. It flickered. In one moment everything was destroyed. In shambles. The magic clearly gone.

But one thing was constant in both images—one person, actually. And this time, Bruno knew who it was.

Mirabel.

Except in this image, his niece was older—wiser. Still a child, but more mature. She seemed confused but also curious in the vision. And there was something about her expression that told Bruno she was essential to whatever was going on.

But would his mami agree? he wondered.

He let out a long sigh as the vision began to fade from his mind.

The reality was, she would not.

She would blame the child—would pour the fear and anxiety that had sprung from the missed gift into her. Mirabel would be miserable. She would never find peace. And though he was sure Alma loved her granddaughter, she could still find room to resent her, as well.

Bruno could not allow that to happen.

But what could he do? he thought. His mother would be at his doorway tomorrow morning—expecting some clarity. An answer. Something to help her form a plan to save Encanto. And all Bruno could give her was a giant arrow pointing at his niece, who was not to blame. If anything, Bruno thought, she would be the Encanto's salvation. But Alma Madrigal didn't want theoreticals. She wanted prophecy. Fact. If Bruno told her that Mirabel was front and center in this dark vision, she wouldn't need to know much more.

The packing took less time than he'd expected. His rucksack was spacious, and he didn't really need much—not where he was going. A few shirts. Padilla's faded, torn cloak. Some food from the pantry. Matches. Some tools. He tied everything together, kept it compact and light. He wasn't going very far, after all.

He couldn't leave a note, and he had to fight the urge to find his hermanas—to tell his twins what was happening. They'd stop him. They'd talk him out of it. They'd tell Mami. No, it was too risky. He would leave and take this vision with him. It was for the best. This gift that had brought so much joy—but also its fair share of torment and sadness—to Encanto was a burden he didn't want to share. The last thing Bruno Madrigal wanted to do was create problems for people he cared about.

Especially Mirabel.

With a slight creak, Bruno stepped into a tiny crevice in the wall of Casita.

He didn't look back.

EPILOGUE

Bruno watched as Mirabel kicked the ball. It rolled into Casita from the front yard, bouncing haphazardly into the foyer. It settled at the foot of the stairs that led up to the house's second floor. The girl followed the ball. She couldn't be older than twelve, and Bruno felt a shock of surprise as he noticed how much she'd grown. Had time passed so fast since he'd decided to leave the family—to hide in the crawl spaces and shadows of Casita, to explore the areas that had only been a temporary refuge for him as a child? Now they were his home. The rats that shared the space with him were his friends. But he'd found some solace here— some peace that he'd believed impossible before. No one was asking for a peek into their future. Alma wasn't looming over him, gently nudging him to be more like anyone else.

He missed his sisters. And his mother. He missed the years he'd lost with his nieces and nephews. He missed his family and the neighborhood and community. But it'd been for the best. In that moment, at least.

Bruno tightened the ruana—Padilla's old cloak—around him and moved the painting to reveal a hole in the wall, a hole large enough for a man to fit through. Surely she couldn't see him, he thought, as he peered down at the foot of the stairs. Mirabel grabbed the ball and stomped up the stairs with a stern determination Bruno found strangely familiar.

She looked so much like her mother, Julieta, he thought as he pulled the painting back slowly, trying not to make a sound. They had the same fierce eyes and determined gait.

"Mirabel," he whispered to himself. A friendly rat scurried up to his shoulder and started to peek out, as well.

"Can't even kick a ball right," Mirabel said under her breath as she tossed the ball toward her room. "Can't change the weather. Can't change shape. Can't cook. I'm just plain ol' Mirabel—no gift, nothing special to offer. Just . . . nobody."

Bruno took in a sharp breath as he watched Mirabel step closer to his hiding spot. His heart felt heavy as he heard her words. He'd known a boy like her, he mused. Even with a supposed gift, he'd felt like an outsider—an outcast with no home, even in a town built by his own family. He wanted to reach out, to hold Mirabel's hand and promise her everything would be fine.

But would it be? he thought.

He watched as Mirabel plopped down, her back against the wall, her shoulder a few inches from the painting. She let out a long, winding sigh.

" 'Don't worry, Mirabel, you're special in your own way,' she tells me," Mirabel said, clearly imitating his sister Julieta. " 'Not everyone receives the gift the same way, mija.' Well, why not?"

Bruno stifled a laugh. Mirabel's imitation was spot-on. The kid had talent. He covered his mouth, trying to minimize any noise, freezing as she looked up toward the painting. Had she heard something? His body tensed, then relaxed as Mirabel's gaze returned to the floor.

"Sometimes I just wish . . . I dunno . . . that I was somewhere else," she said softly. Bruno couldn't see her face, but he didn't need to. He heard her sniffling. "Where it didn't matter if I had a gift, or if I was special. I just want to be appreciated for who I am. Not who I was supposed to be, or whatever people think I'm supposed to be."

"You are special."

The words escaped Bruno's mouth before he could stop himself. He waited, unmoving, expecting her to react. But she didn't. She hadn't heard him.

He let out a brief sigh, turning to face another of his rats that sat next to him, watching him closely.

"I wish I could yell it to her," Bruno said softly. "I want her to know she is special. She is loved."

The rat squeaked sharply in response.

Bruno watched as Mirabel got closer to the painting—too close. He needed to create some distance. He knew himself too well. He wouldn't be able to stop himself from speaking to her.

Bruno scurried up a ladder and around a tunnel, panting heavily, watching where he could to keep tabs on Mirabel. He couldn't risk her finding him. But he didn't want to leave her like this. Even if he couldn't say anything to her, he could at least make sure she wasn't totally alone—even if she didn't know he was there.

He stopped at the ceiling and brought his face close to the bottom, where he could see Mirabel through a long crack. He spoke through the crack, his mouth close to the floor he'd been walking on. Two of his rats were next to him now, watching Bruno talk to Mirabel in whispers only he could hear.

"Don't be afraid," Bruno said, his voice a low, fleeting whisper. "Please, don't worry, Mirabel."

He watched as Mirabel continued to pace, caught up in her own world, completely unaware that her uncle was looking down on her, cheering her on.

He wanted to say more, even if she couldn't hear—but it was a bad idea.

Bruno's gut told him to stop, to leave things, lest he be discovered. But something else kept him where he was, watching his young niece bouncing around his old house, and he tried to suss out what was going on. He wanted to be there for her in a way no one had been there for him. To tell her she'd be fine. To tell her it was okay to be weird—to be different—to embrace it and enjoy it. To tap into the purest feeling of being herself, not trying to meet someone else's preconceived notions of what she should be. But how could he do that now, through so many walls and layers, through so much baggage and history?

His mind drifted back, to years ago. To Roberto. To that dark night just a few feet from where he and Mirabel stood now. To a time when Bruno had been twisted and manipulated, pulled away from himself and used as a tool against his own family—his own home. He wouldn't allow that to happen to anyone else, much less Mirabel.

He backed away from the ceiling and watched as Mirabel slowly wandered outside, still seeming unmoored. Bruno walked deeper into the bowels of Casita's tunnels with a plan.

ᘓᘀᘓᘀᘓᘀᘓᘀ

Mirabel saw the rat scurrying out of her room and almost screamed, but she stopped herself. It was just a rat, she thought. Just one of a million different kinds of animals she saw every day in Encanto.

But there was something weird about this one, she thought.

She let the thought linger with her for a moment longer before she entered her room. She had other things on her mind. Her grandmother, Alma, had just chastised her for something and it had irked Mirabel. Not because she hadn't done anything wrong—she had totally tripped Isabela—but because she didn't feel like being disciplined by her abuela. She was tired of being compared to everyone else in the family, everyone who had gifts of their own to wave around.

She made a beeline for her bed and plopped down with a sigh. She was tired and frustrated. She knew this. Everything was setting her off lately. Years had passed since the ceremony when Mirabel thought she would get her gift and nothing had materialized. Maybe she just wasn't special, she thought. Maybe she was meant to be like this. Her parents still loved her, true. Her sisters did, as well, in their own way. Abuela Alma did, too, she was sure—even if she treated Mirabel like a freak who could uproot everything in Encanto. Y'know, no big deal.

She heard the crinkling of paper on her bed. Had she left something here before heading to school?

She got up and spun around. In the spot where she'd sat, Mirabel spied a small folded-up sheet of paper. It was from her abuela's office—but the handwriting was most definitely not Alma's. Mirabel unfolded it slowly, then read the longhand message.

You are special. You are loved. You will do great things.

The letter was unsigned. Mirabel's first thought was to toss it away, but for some reason she held it to her chest. Her face grew hot. A few minutes later, a few tears streaked down her cheeks.

It didn't matter who'd written it. It might not even be intended for her. The rat could've brought it from anywhere, she knew. But she also believed in signs, and she believed in things happening for a reason. The reality was, Mirabel had needed to see those words today, of all days. Whoever had written them at least understood what Mirabel was experiencing in her heart, even if they didn't know *her*—and that was more than she could say for her own family and friends. The note reminded her that she was unique and special on her own terms, not in relation to Encanto, her family, or a gift. Maybe they'd been through something similar themself.

Mirabel wiped away her tears and gently refolded the paper. She slipped it into the drawer where she kept her special things. She sat in silence for a moment, wondering what to do next.

Then she sprang to her feet and walked out—eager to seize the future.